It is with great fondness and deep appreciation that we dedicate this book to AMINAH BRENDA LYNN ROBINSON (1940-2015), American artist, for her inspiration and encouragement.

A.L.M. & D.B.

Loukas
and the
Game of Chance

www.mascotbooks.com

Loukas and the Game of Chance

For more information, please contact:
Mascot Books
620 Herndon Parkway, Suite 320
Herndon, VA 20170
info@mascotbooks.com

Library of Congress Control Number: 2018904432

CPSIA Code: PRTWP0419A
ISBN-13: 978-1-68401-433-0

Printed in South Korea

Loukas
and the
Game of Chance

Anthony L. Manna

Illustrated by Donald Babisch

In a time long ago forgotten, a fisherman, his wife, and their son lived peacefully together on a remote island in the restless Aegean Sea. Their weathered cottage stood on a cliff overlooking clusters of drab villages scattered throughout wooded hills.

Paths overgrown with wild herbs and gnarled shrubs wended their way from the family's cottage down to the island's busy harbor.

For generations the cottage and the plot of land on which it stood with its commanding view of the sea had remained a cherished inheritance. Over the years, each family that lived there took great pride in preserving the humble beauty of the place.

Like his ancestors before him, the fisherman believed it was in his honor to pass the skills of the fishing trade to his child. From time to time, he would bring his young son along when he headed out to sea in the family's old row boat.

On days when the boy joined his father, he woke to his mother's call as darkness was draining from the night sky. He dressed himself just like his father—in overalls, clunky rubber boots, and a scruffy cap.

Before setting out, the boy was sure to grab the wooden flute his parents had made for him to celebrate his christening and to honor the spirit of Saint Loukas, the legendary miracle worker whose name the boy had been given at birth.

Just as Loukas was about to rush off to meet up with his father on the path, his mother handed him the small sack of food she had prepared for their outing. With the family's pantry nearly empty each and every day, she could only offer Loukas and his father a few slices of bread and a small wedge of cheese to share.

As daylight was brightening, Loukas and his father boarded their boat and rowed out to a shallow channel not far beyond the shore. There they waited for schools of sardines and mullets to fill their net.

Whenever Loukas accompanied his father out to sea, he helped pass the time out on the water by taking up his flute and playing sea songs.

They never tired of hearing the song that honored a trawler's captain and crew for fighting off a band of pirates on the high seas.

Or the song about the islanders' lament for fisherfolk lost at sea during a brutal storm.

Or the children's song that captured the playful spirit of dolphins as they rode a schooner's bow waves.

Or the songs of mermaids and merlads, sea monsters, and legendary sirens whose singing lured unwary sailors to steer their boats onto rocks that lined the coast.

On days when good luck guided their boat, Loukas and his father returned to the dock by midday with a basket, full to the brim, of fish. Later, Loukas would help his parents sell the day's catch at the village marketplace along with the herbs the family grew in their modest garden.

As a young boy, Loukas had his father's deep-set sea-green eyes and narrow nose with a slight curve at the bridge.

He also bore his father's slightly crooked smile that, were it not for the man's friendly manner, might easily be mistaken for an angry scowl.

From his mother, Loukas had received an untamed crop of curly black hair and a dark complexion, as though blessed by the sun's golden rays.

Lately, Loukas had taken to imitating the confidence his mother radiated whenever she made her way through their village. As she moved from place to place, folks took kindly to her gentle way of finding goodness in people.

Like Loukas's father, his mother steered clear of gossip that too often poisoned the village with spells of spite and distrust. Even when Loukas was

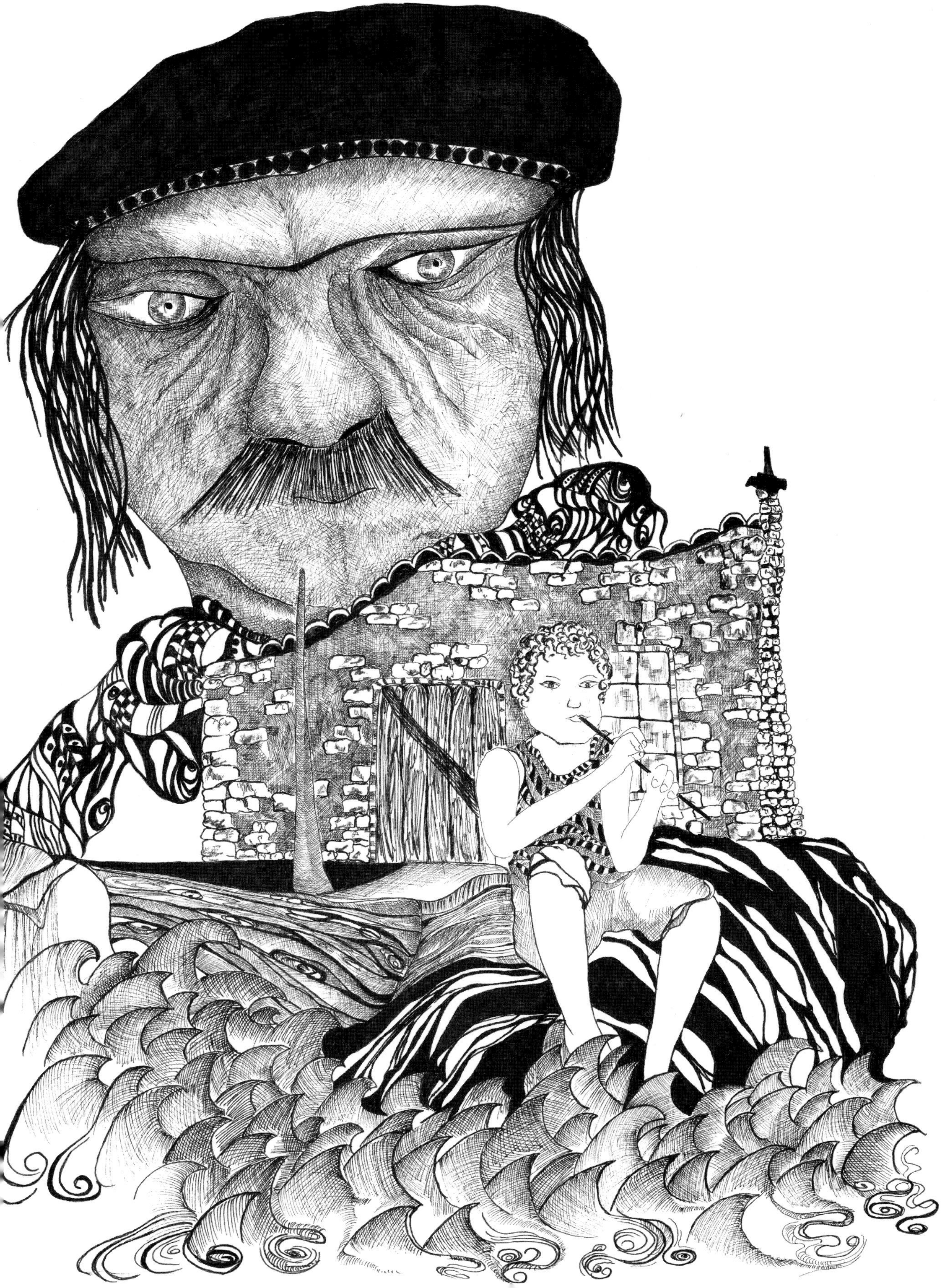

still a young child, his mother warned him to walk away from mean people who talked about folks with spiteful words. Loukas must be kind to people. He must look out for villagers—whether young or old—who need help.

Some days Loukas roamed the seashore alone not far from home. He ran alongside sandpipers as they scuttled across the beach, their shrill cries stirring up a rowdy chorus of weet-weet-weeting.

"awawawk," Loukas screeched, echoing the gulls' calls. He flapped his arms and swayed like an anxious seabird, circling and diving through salty gusts of wind.

"awawawk, awawawk," he cried, and took off down the sun-drenched trail that brought him to the island's ancient seawall.

Once there, Loukas clambered up to a narrow hollow where he took a seat and watched the flurry of activity that swarmed the harbor. By day, merchants from near and far came ashore hoping to sell their wares to the island's eager vendors and shopkeepers.

From his perch, Loukas could see trawlers and tall ships moving to and from the harbor. Flocks of squawking gulls soared and plummeted above the boats' misty wakes, their webbed feet barely touching the sea's churning surface.

As was his habit, Loukas soon began playing a cheerful tune on his flute. He slowed or quickened the rhythm to keep pace with the gulls' sweeping movements. Just when he started mounting a rapid series of high notes, out of the corner of his eye he spotted a snake weaving its way toward him.

Loukas played on, slowly turning to catch a glimpse of his visitor. This snake looked just like the snakes Loukas and his friends came upon in the island's rocky hillsides. From the snake's markings, Loukas could tell it was a leopard snake.

Islanders welcomed leopard snakes into their gardens. From ancient tales came the belief that leopard snakes brought good luck to households. Because their fangs dripped no venom, leopard snakes were favored as pets throughout the island.

In the bright sunlight, the snake's silver scales glowed with a trail of dark-edged, reddish-brown stripes. Close to each of these marks was a black splotch that made Loukas think of little shields protecting the snake from its enemies.

Of all the snake's features Loukas could see at first glance, it was the snake's eyes that held the boy spellbound. The eyes—large, round, and black—stared so intently into Loukas's own eyes he wondered if the snake was trying to search his thoughts.

The snake came to a sudden stop at Loukas's feet and slowly raised its thick body to its full height. It stood on its wiry tail and swayed from side to side in harmony with the changing pulse of Loukas's surging rhythms.

Loukas slowed the tempo and brought the song through its final measures. At once, the snake sank to the ground and slithered across the same stony path that had led it to the boy and the delightful sounds of his flute. Before retreating to its shelter, it twisted its head around and peered at Loukas, its tongue flickering a steady beat.

Once the snake had slipped away, Loukas drew in a deep breath at what he saw on the path before him. In its wake, the snake had left behind a gift of not one, not two, but *three* gold coins that shimmered in the sun's brilliant light.

Loukas called out a "thank you" to the snake.

"My prayers have been answered," Loukas said aloud while making the sign of the cross. Like his mother and father, he often prayed for an end to the suffering the family was made to endure with only a few pennies to see them through each and every day.

The snake's gift means there will be enough food on the table and an end to our aching stomachs, Loukas thought.

It meant his mother could repair her stall at the village market where she sold fish and herbs.

It meant his father could buy supplies to overhaul his row boat and replace the worn oars.

It meant his family could mend the chinks in the cottage walls and patch the cottage's crumbling foundation.

It meant they could return the kindness of neighbors who had come to the family's rescue when their pantry had gone empty and only a few fish had made it into their baskets. Now they could reach out to neighbors who needed their help to survive. It could be his family's mission.

In less time than it takes to blink an eye, Loukas wrapped the coins in the cloth he used for wiping down his flute. He then grabbed his things and sped down the trail to the dock where he waited for his father's return.

Loukas's heart was nearly bursting with excitement from anticipating his parents' surprise when they would first lay eyes on the snake's precious offering.

The second his father stepped onto the dock, Loukas rushed headlong into his story about meeting up with the snake. Not once did he take a breath until he came to the part where the snake had left in its wake not one, not two, but *three* gold coins.

When Loukas's story ended, the two hurried off to their cottage to bring the news to Loukas's mother.

"As fate would have it," the father announced, all the while unfolding the cloth that held the treasure with trembling hands, "the spell cast by our son's music has brought us a stroke of good luck.

"Oh, my son," Loukas's father continued, "on this wonderful day, your gift of music has touched our lives with a special blessing."

"Let us offer a prayer of thanks," Loukas's mother said.

Seconds later, Loukas joined his mother and father at the makeshift altar that stood in a corner of their cottage. They knelt before the small statue of Saint Loukas, the family's protector, that stood on the altar.

"Saint Loukas, holy guardian, please accept our gratitude for the help you have brought to us today," Loukas's father prayed.

"We share with you our endless gratitude for giving us the means to survive," said Loukas's mother.

"And for the snake," Loukas added. "Praise the snake that found its way to my music. That gave to me *three* gold coins and a better life for my family."

"Amen," they said together.

"If your luck holds out and the snake comes by the seawall to be entertained by you once again," Loukas's mother said to her son, "be sure to play a song to let the snake know how deeply grateful our family is for helping us pull through these difficult times."

Early the next morning, as soon as Loukas settled into his seawall lookout and began playing a string of simple chords, the snake emerged from its burrow and slithered over to where Loukas sat. It raised itself taller and taller and stood within arm's length of Loukas's stare. The snake held Loukas steady in its sight.

As before, the snake caught hold of Loukas's soothing riffs. It swayed from side to side and pitched forward and backward, weaving its way into the rise and fall of the music's rhythms.

As soon as Loukas quickened the tune's tempo and ended with high-pitched trills, the snake lowered itself to the ground and slid off to its den.

Once again, Loukas stood amazed at the sight of not one, not two, but *three* gold coins the snake had left along the path.

"Thank you, my friend," Loukas cried out to the snake.

"From now on, I will call you 'Lambros,'" Loukas said out loud. "The name means 'radiant,' and radiant is the kindness you have brought to me and my family."

Loukas dropped the coins into his bag and ran off singing, "Laaaam...bros, Laaaam...bros, Laaaam... bros." He was happy to be bringing home more good news.

"Your snake has rescued us from a life of poverty," Loukas's father remarked when his son returned from a meeting with the snake bearing yet another share of Lambros's generosity.

"And we are just as thankful to you, my son, for giving your mysterious friend such great pleasure with your pleasing music," said his mother.

Again and again, Loukas returned to the seawall to play his flute to Lambros's delight.

Again and again, Lambros rewarded Loukas with not one, not two, but *three* gold coins.

Some years later, just as spring's first traces were awakening the island's hillsides and meadows with a dazzling palette of orange and lemon blossoms, Lambros spoke to Loukas.

Loukas smiled to hear Lambros's gravelly voice. *Not only does this wondrous snake dance,* he thought, *it also speaks our language.*

"My friend," the snake said in a voice so strained it seemed each slurred word came from within a deep well. "Someday I will be called from this earthly realm to return to the spirit world and join up with members of my clan who have passed on before me."

Loukas struggled to hear Lambros's every word above the harbor's commotion.

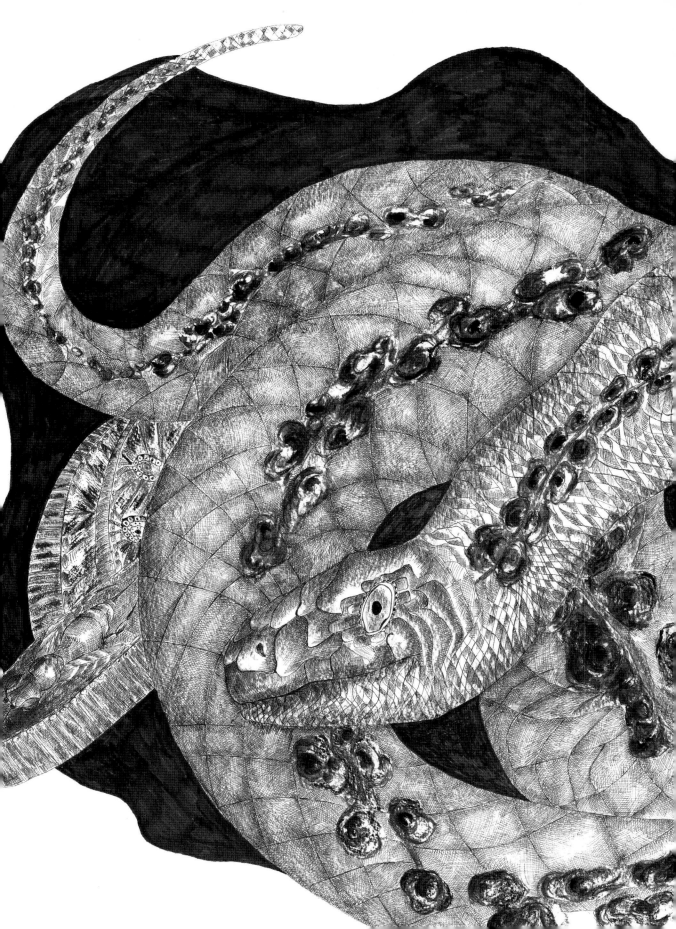

"You will help ease my journey and keep my spirit from ceaseless roaming between this world and the world beyond if you give me a respectful burial," Lambros said.

Nodding in agreement, Loukas clutched his hands against his chest.

"When you find my body in my hideaway," Lambros continued, his voice weakening, "wrap it in a white cloth and put me to rest in a grave that looks out to the sea I love.

"In friendship, bury me with a sprig of sage to protect me from wicked powers that may threaten my spirit as I make my passage."

His voice trembling with sadness at the thought of losing his friend, Loukas stammered through a promise to keep close to his heart Lambros's wish to be helped bringing his spirit home.

"Your companionship comforts me as much as your music awakens me to great happiness," rasped the snake. His hoarse voice faded to a sluggish tremor as he slipped out of sight.

Loukas gazed after Lambros through tearful eyes.

Over the years, as Loukas's friendship with Lambros blossomed, so, too, his family's fortune.

Where once they were too poor even to come by a few cents to buy flour to make bread, with time they had become one of the richest families on the island.

With Lambros's coins filling their strongbox, Loukas's family rejoiced over the changes their new wealth brought into their lives.

They built a new cottage with an unrivaled view of the sea.

They planted spacious flower, herb, and vegetable gardens.

They brought onto their homestead a small herd of goats.

They installed a marble fountain.

They hollowed out a tract for a pond.

They planted chestnut trees as a tribute to Lambros for his good will and devotion.

In honor of Lambros, Loukas's family came to the aid of the village's poorest folks. Along with his mother and father, Loukas left baskets of food at the doorways of villagers most in need of help. At every season, they brought clothing made by the village seamstress to families troubled by poor health and hard times.

Before long, a band of neighbors grew curious about the surprising turn of good fortune Loukas's family had taken—and so quickly, at that!

When neither Loukas nor his mother or father said a word to anyone about the source of their blessings for fear of losing the snake's trust, their neighbors' curiosity soured into jealousy.

"Look how they make a spectacle of themselves," one neighbor confided to folks passing through the village square one afternoon. He gestured toward the lavish cottage the family had built on one of the island's highest bluffs.

"Indeed," agreed a milliner, stopping in the square on the way to her shop. "Word is out that they've hired a crew of caretakers to look after their place.

"Pity us who must fend for ourselves day after day," she said, a look of disgust pinching her face as she minced out of the square.

"Not to mention the gardeners they bring in to care for their cypress and olive trees. Those trees are unequal to any others on the entire island," another villager observed, sulking.

As rumors about the family's wealth raged on with each passing year, Loukas never once allowed the villagers' envy to force him to reveal his friendship with Lambros. Nor did Loukas ever consider putting an end to cheering the snake on with songs that invited him to dance.

Lambros could no longer move as nimbly as he had years before when first coming to trust the young boy at the seawall. Yet, even as he aged, the snake was drawn out of his den the minute the stirring sounds of Loukas's flute came to him on the drift of a gentle sea breeze.

As Loukas came within months of his eighteenth birthday, his features still held the same wide-eyed curiosity he had carried throughout his youth. Framed by a shock of tangly black hair, his face bore a perpetual tan. His green eyes were darker. These were eyes that glanced about for fear of missing out on whatever was happening within his line of vision.

Loukas was more likely to be found smiling shyly than frowning. While his short, thickset body stood firmly grounded, he always appeared restless and weightless, as though ready to spring into action the moment the need arose.

On the very day Loukas celebrated his eighteenth birthday, his mother and father announced that Thera, a young and beautiful seamstress, had gladly accepted Loukas's offer to marry him.

Thera had a thick thatch of wavy blond hair and lightly lashed bright blue eyes. "Thera's eyes," Loukas told his friends, "are as blue as the sea."

Thera often pulled her hair back from her face. She kept it in place behind her ears with a silver barrette inlaid with amber gemstones. The barrette was a gift from her grandmother.

Like her father, Thera was tall and slim. Like her mother, she had a pale complexion and long, thin fingers ideal for a seamstress's work. From her mother, she had a nose with a straight bridge and narrow nostrils.

Islanders were drawn to Thera's shop. They said she always treated her customers with respect, took special care in making and mending their clothes, and was known for putting a fair price on their finished pieces.

Thera loved music. Islanders passed by her shop, often stopping to listen to her singing songs that told of love and loss and forgiveness.

As it happened, Thera's sister brought to Loukas's family her mother and father's approval of Thera's marriage to Loukas. Her sister announced that the families would soon meet to issue a formal agreement as to the suitability of the couple's union. They would discuss the terms and duration of the courtship. Thera's dowry would be decided. The family the married couple would live with would be debated, and the village priest would be called upon to bless the union.

Dare I ask Lambros if someday soon I might invite Thera to the seawall and introduce her to my faithful friend? Loukas gave thought to what he might say the next time he came to the seawall to charm the snake.

When Loukas returned to the seawall a few days later, Lambros rose up slowly to meet Loukas's eyes. As though reading Loukas's thoughts, Lambros whispered: "Surely, my man, it would greatly please me to make the acquaintance of the young woman who has chosen you above all others to be her husband." His gritty voice was so quiet Loukas struggled to catch hold of each word.

"And when she accompanies you to this place, ask each of your parents to join the two of you," wheezed Lambros.

Some days passed before Loukas could lead Thera and their parents to the seawall where they waited at Loukas's watch for the snake to appear. Once they settled in, Loukas played the seafaring ballad that over time had become one of Lambros's favorite songs.

But this time, something was different.

Loukas hastened the tempo, but even then, Lambros did not emerge from his shelter.

Seconds later, Loukas and the others started searching the seawall for the snake's whereabouts. Coming to a gap, they struggled to set aside a pile of rocks that blocked all but a small section of the opening.

Loukas and Thera used their hands to scoop away a mound of loose dirt from the opening. Once they pushed the dirt aside, they discovered a large pit. Peering into the pit, they saw Lambros's coiled body lying lifeless on a stretch of rocky ground.

When their calls to the snake failed to rouse him, they knew he was dead.

"Even in death, this snake is a beautiful creation," said Loukas's mother when Loukas and Thera laid Lambros's body on a grassy clearing near the seawall.

"A blessing from nature," Thera's father said as he passed over Lambros with the sign of the cross.

"To our family, a savior," Loukas's father said, nearly in tears.

That evening as daylight ebbed into dusk, Loukas gathered with Thera and the couple's parents to bury Lambros. With hearts heavy with grief, Loukas and Thera dug a grave close to the towering chestnut tree that grew a short distance from their cottage. The grave faced the sea, as Lambros had wished.

Loukas honored Lambros's other request by shrouding the snake's body in fine white linen. He lowered Lambros into the grave and cast several sprigs of sage over the body.

"May this offering of sage protect our snake on his journey into the spirit world," Loukas said.

After the grave was filled, Loukas, Thera, and the others raised their hands toward the heavens and sent Lambros's spirit off. They felt a deep sense of gratitude toward the snake for having freed them from a life of hardship.

Beginning that day, Loukas and Thera lived a charmed life. In time, the couple brought into the world two children, first a girl they named Sophie, and a year later, a boy they named Petros.

By the time Sophie celebrated her tenth birthday, she had wavy blond hair like her mother and dark green eyes like her father. Her warm, welcoming smile was comforting to folks, both young and old alike.

"Like a dancer she moves," villagers commented when they watched Sophie running through the village square with her school friends.

At nine years old, Petros was beginning to favor his father's solid square build and thick, dark eyebrows. His curly hair was as black and wild as his father's, and his blue eyes were as bright as his mother's.

Like his father, Petros learned to master the flute. Ever since he could hold the instrument, his mother's guidance had given him confidence and his father's lessons had shown him how to play the instrument with great skill.

From their parents, Sophie and Petros had learned to speak kindly of people.

"Better to say nothing at all about someone than speak ill of that person with cruel words," their mother often reminded them.

"Cruel words make people suffer," their father would say. "Remember to hold your tongue and walk away from nasty gossip."

As fate would have it one stormy spring day, Loukas met up with his friends for a game of cards at a local seaside cafe.

Joining the game was a crafty merchant. He was a hateful man who took great pleasure from spreading rumors about islanders he despised. The merchant was fond of telling his patrons that Loukas, their wealthiest neighbor, gained his riches from illegal trading off the island.

As the card game wore on, Loukas and his friends kept losing their bids to the merchant's winning hands.

"My luck is down," his friend Demetri said upon showing his third losing hand to the merchant's straight flush. He bowed out of the game and left the cafe.

"I haven't a chance of breaking even," said Nikos, Loukas's other friend. When the merchant won the pot with a royal flush, Nikos quit the game and walked out of the cafe without a word.

Loukas stayed on. His rage mounted as he brought to mind the merchant's lies about trade deals that called into question his honesty.

"Well, my good man, I see you have more faith in your skill than those two cowards," the merchant said. He nodded toward the cafe door with a sly grin.

"My turn to deal," Loukas muttered. He glared at the merchant. His cheeks flushed. He was short of breath, and he was working up a sweat.

The game soon heated to a fierce contest.

I must defeat this scoundrel, Loukas thought. *He has disgraced me and defaced my family's name.*

"Play on, play on," the merchant urged.

The merchant stood. He brought his fists close to his face. He narrowed his eyes to stare at his opponent.

The bets increased with higher stakes, and Loukas kept losing.

Loukas's desire to turn the game to his favor blurred his thinking.

He soon began gambling away the many riches Lambros's generosity had brought into his family.

He lost his treasured cottage and the large tract of land on a hillside that opened to a view of the sea.

He lost the goats.

Next, the statue-laced fountains and lush gardens that surrounded the cottage went to the merchant.

In the next round, all that remained of Loukas's treasures were his wife and children.

He could see the madness in sacrificing his family to satisfy a hunger for defeating his rival.

He could flee from the game if it meant saving his beloved Thera and their children.

What should he do? What *did* he do?

Loukas worked himself into such a frenzy over crushing the merchant that he lost the will to quit the game.

When he laid down his next hand showing two pairs of aces over tens, the merchant trumped him with four of a kind.

Loukas had no choice but to hand over the lives he loved.

Dazed, he forced himself from the table, nearly toppling it.

Shame blazed through him.

He navigated a clumsy about face, grabbed his satchel, and staggered out of the cafe.

The merchant's shrill laughter followed Loukas as he stumbled onto the rugged roadway that led from the harbor up into the forested highlands.

Like a sleepwalker, Loukas trudged on. He was nearly bursting with anger over his recklessness.

With his heart breaking from his losses, he came to an abrupt stop and raised his fists skyward.

"Before God, the saints, and the sacred spirits that rule the Earth, I vow to free my family from the curse my madness has inflicted on us all," Loukas cried out in anguish.

At that very moment, he recalled a legend that told of islanders going in search of Destiny to seek release from the suffering fate had handed them to test their will to survive.

Like those islanders, he must gather his courage and go off to find Destiny somewhere deep within the island forest where she lived with her son Ilion, the Sun, and her daughter Luna, the Moon.

He would plead with Destiny for the right to salvage his honor, his fortune, and—"please, please, please," he begged—his enslaved family's freedom.

Just as twilight began spreading its melancholy glow over the island, Loukas stood at a fork in the road. He was pondering which direction he should take to find Destiny when he caught sight of a curious cart. It was

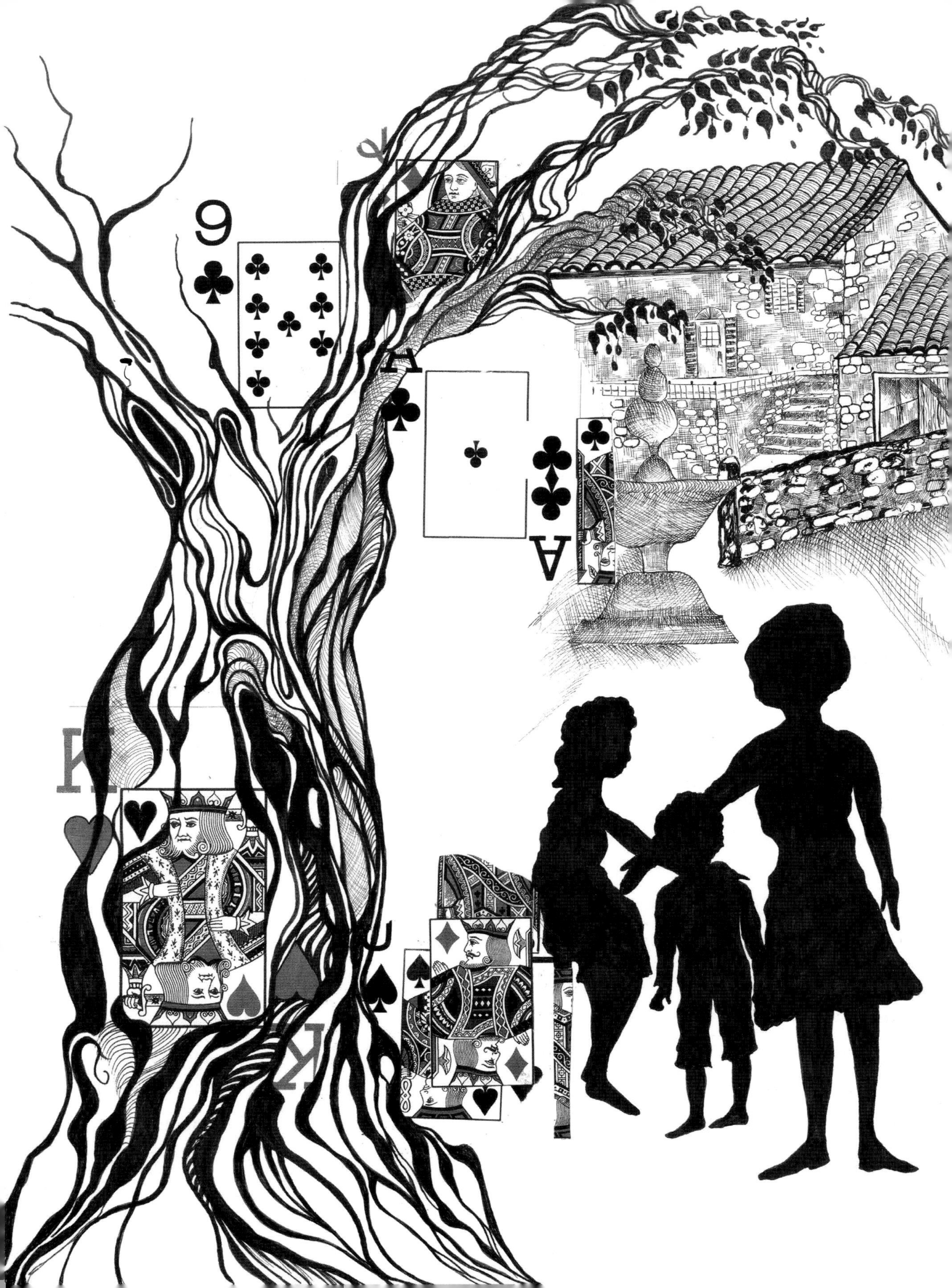

parked near the path that led into the forest.

From a distance, Loukas could see that the cart was made of roughly-hewn crooked branches. Potted plants and an old barrel and trunk took up most of its bed. A wooden rake, a broom, and a shovel, each with a knobby handle were tied to a wooden slat attached to one side of the cart.

The cart was painted in dark red, blue, yellow, and purple. The bright colors reminded Loukas of carts he'd seen in carnivals and festivals throughout the island.

Loukas moved cautiously toward the cart to get a better view of it. A few steps later, he spotted a leather banner spread across a branch above the rear of the cart. A smile spread across Loukas's face as he made out the words on the banner. "Keeper of the Forest," he read and bobbed his head, amused.

At once, memories of Keeper of the Forest rushed through his thoughts. Keeper was the brave character in age-old stories that had enchanted Loukas throughout his childhood. In an instant, Loukas pictured Keeper setting off on yet another exciting mission in the island's northern forest.

Keeper was an adventurer who was known for roaming the forest to fend off wicked creatures and spirits. Keeper could also be counted on to come up with the best plans for settling conflicts among forest animals and for helping to keep the forest fertile.

And now Loukas stood next to a cart claimed by the story character he had come to idolize. Loukas's smile widened. Could his fearless childhood hero be *real? Flesh-and-blood real?*

A high-pitched voice startled Loukas out of his musing. He struggled to understand the speaker's peculiar drawl.

"Hey, yah, ho. You thar," the voice called from within a stand of poplars. "On thees road forsaken thou art traveling. From whom or what ah do thou flee? Thees forsaken road whar even the seabirds rarhrley fly, thou boldly walk on by."

"Honorable one, I mean no harm and bear no evil," Loukas stammered while he surveyed the poplars.

"Hey, yah, ho. Looky thou up and up," the voice squealed. "Heeee, heeee, heeee. Keeper of the Forest plants. Keeper of the Forest sows. Keeper of the Forest knows all. Heeee, heeee, heeee. Looky up and up ah."

Loukas shrieked with delight. "Keeper lives. Keeper is *real*. Keeper's stories are true."

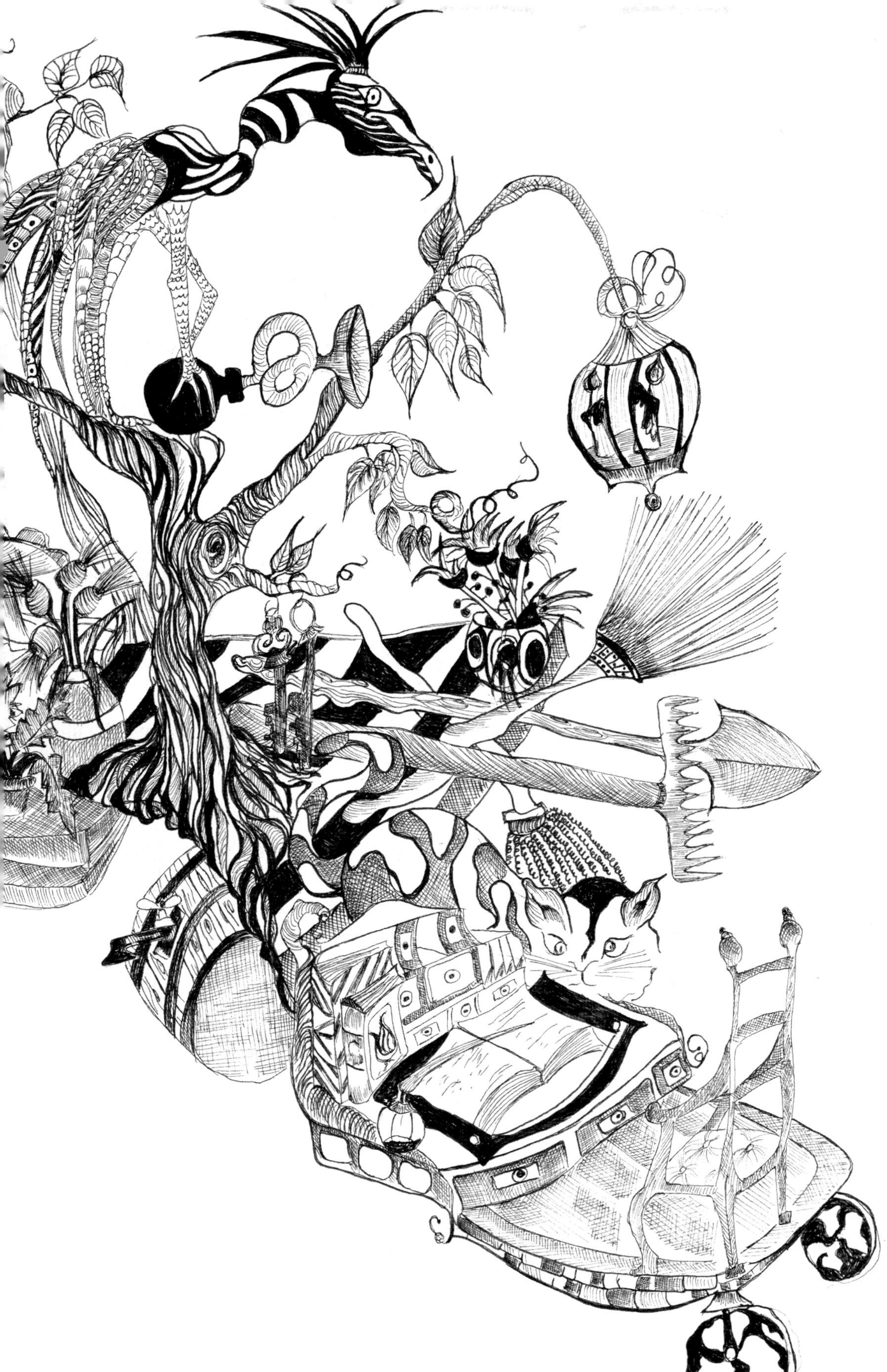

Loukas stepped closer to the poplars and gazed upward, trembling. He moved wide-eyed from tree to tree in the deepening dusk. His heart thumped hard on his chest.

Keeper's whistling drew Loukas to one of the tallest trees. He steadied himself against the trunk and slowly gazed upward. As Keeper's figure came into focus, Loukas let out a muffled cry.

"Oh, my, oh, my," Loukas exclaimed once Keeper's image cleared.

Keeper stood on a thick branch and whistled a string of high and low pitches. Up above his head, Keeper held an odd double-tiered umbrella mounted on a narrow pole. The umbrella's large, open canopy topped the pole. Directly under that canopy there was a smaller canopy. It also was open. The ribs that supported both canopies were thin metal pipes. Puffs of colored smoke erupted from the pipes in rapid spurts.

"Poooofsss, poooofsss, pooofsssssss," sounded the smoke at its release.

At the end of each pipe, there hung a tassel with a large bell attached to it. The bells rang when the canopies took to spinning; the top canopy clockwise, the bottom one counter clockwise. For both, it was a wobbly ride.

The spinning stopped abruptly. Keeper made a piercing whistle sound. At once, a volley of belches, hiccups, squeaks, hoots, and squawks came from somewhere inside the umbrella.

"Heeee, heeee, heeee," Keeper sang. Like a high-wire performer, he teetered forward a few steps on the branch, stopped, and staggered backward. He soon came to a shaky pause, stepped off the branch, and floated gently downward, whistling. He landed in a clearing a few feet from Loukas.

Keeper looked just like the character Loukas had imagined many years ago in stories told of Keeper's daring deeds.

Indeed, Keeper was the same earthy character in tales Loukas and Thera now enjoyed telling Sophie and Petros, their own children.

Keeper was muscular and squat. His skin was the color of spring fern, and

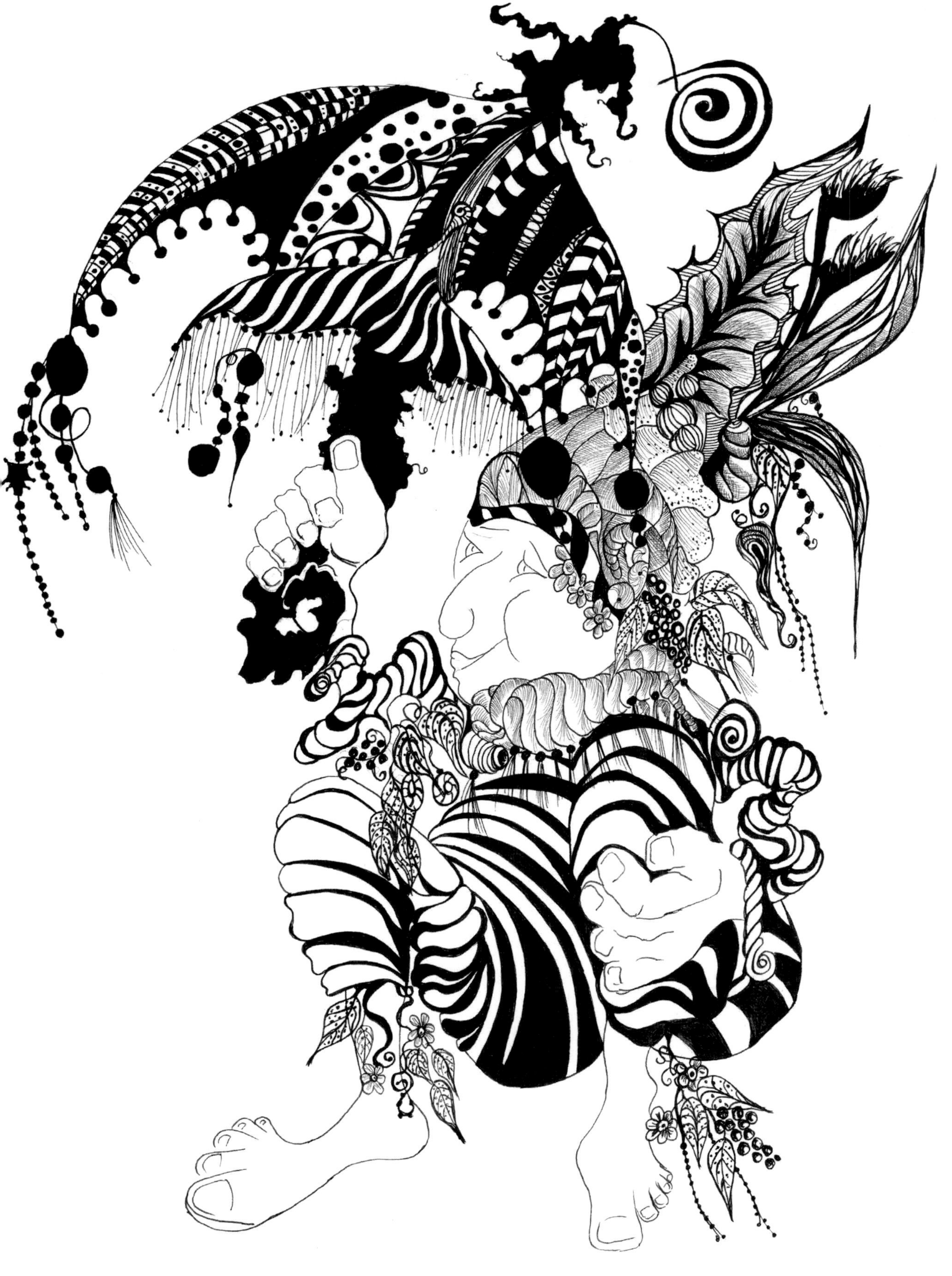

he had very large hands and feet from which sprouted weeds and grasses. A patch of moss covered Keeper's head. Out of the moss grew berries, buds, and blossoms.

Keeper wore clothes styled with wide, horizontal stripes in shades of leaf greens, earth browns, and sunlight yellows. Leafy vines trailed out from underneath a loose-fitting jacket and pants.

"Whar art thou bound dah?" drawled Keeper.

"Venerable Keeper, I have taken to this road in search of Destiny," Loukas said. "Now that my foolishness has brought me down, it is her wisdom I am seeking to show me how to mend my broken heart and turn my ruined life around."

"Ah, ah. Destiny, Destiny," Keeper cried. "Oh, har favor not so easily gained dah. Mortal upon mortal have passed thees way desperate for Destiny's cure," continued Keeper. "Just as many have returned more, oooh, more and more wretched than when they set out tah. Crestfallen wahr they for having failed to receive Destiny's guidance to change the course of thar tormented lives sah."

Keeper drew closer to Loukas, and with deep-set eyes studied Loukas's expression. The adventurer knew at once that no warning could ever dampen this mortal's desire to find Destiny and plead with her to free him from his misery.

"To gain Destiny's patronage, thy request must first be judged dah worthy by har son Ilion, the Sun, and har daughter Luna, the Moon," Keeper confided while moving within inches of Loukas's stunned face.

"Only then will a decision be made if thy fate deserves the attention thou crave. Oh, and oh, and oh," said Keeper, sighing.

Keeper warned Loukas that he must tread cautiously if he should ever come into the company of Destiny, Luna, and Ilion.

"But why, honored Keeper?" asked Loukas.

"Ah, young mahn, many are the tales Highland folk tell of Ilion's unpredictable mood when he returns to the palace from his daily rounds at day's end dah," Keeper said.

"If Sun returns troubled by what has happened among the mortals that day, you had better bewhar. Oh and ah, Sun might just as easily consume thee with a hellish fire than urge his mother to take notice of thy petition," Keeper predicted.

"As far Luna," cautioned Keeper, "if she becomes troubled from witnessing the mortals immersed in strife, har wrath ah could force har to bewitch thee with a horrifying spell. Woe, woe, woe."

That said, Keeper pointed his umbrella toward the forest and directed Loukas to follow the path northward.

Well into his travels, Keeper told Loukas he would come to a radiant vermilion palace where Destiny and her son and daughter have lived since the beginning of earthly time.

"Along the way, thou will arrive at a steep bluff Highlanders call Ravens Peak," Keeper said. "A short distance from thar, be prepahred to meet up with anguished souls. Sad, so sad. Like thee, my good mahn, they are in need of Destiny's help. Yes, so it will be.

"Oh, spahr thyself a pound of grief, oh, so, by consoling these suffering creatures. Leave them each with a promise. Tell them thou will lay thar requests at the feet of Destiny, Luna, and Ilion. Thou will beg the all-knowing, all-wise Mother, Daughter, and Son to help these needy ones endure their struggles."

Loukas gave Keeper a quizzical look while he gestured his agreement.

"Go, now, go on and on. Follow the pahth ah into the forest's depths. May courage be thy compass, caution thy guide, and good fortune thy reward," Keeper sang.

Keeper tossed the umbrella onto the bed of the cart and took hold of the cart's handle. "Heeee, heeee, heeee. Keeper of the Forest plants. Keeper of the Forest sows. Keeper of the Forest knows all. Heeee, heeee, heeee," the adventurer cried.

Keeper then steered the cart down the forest path at a quickening pace. Soon the cart rose inches above the ground and drove Keeper into the darkness. Seconds later, the moon rolled out from behind a cluster of clouds, offering Loukas a shaft of eerie light to guide him onto the forest's pathway.

All through the night, Loukas cowered at the yelps and cries, the baying and shrieking of restless animals that grew startled by his heavy footfalls. Suddenly, a rush of winged creatures circling overhead sent Loukas running down the path far from their harsh squeals.

Hours later, the first streaks of light dappled the path. As Loukas drew nearer to a broad chain of jagged cliffs, flocks of jet-black ravens soared and glided on gentle breezes. Their loud, throaty croaking pierced the dawn's stillness.

Here is Ravens Peak, the very bluff Keeper had told of, Loukas thought.

Not far beyond the bluff's steep rock face, a woman's screams drew Loukas into a misty clearing.

Once he moved past a narrow bend, he spied three young ladies flailing about. Each threw handfuls of dirt onto flames racing through a pile of brush that stood within reach of a wooden cottage.

At once, Loukas sped to the water trough that stood nearby the cottage. With bucketsful of water, he doused the fire within minutes.

When the danger had passed, the ladies thanked Loukas for his kindness.

Loukas gaped at the ladies in wonder. The strange white gloss of their complexions roused his curiosity.

"May my sisters and I inquire as to what brings you to this forsaken place where even swallows rarely fly by?" the sister with wild crimson hair asked.

"I am on my way to seek the healing powers of Destiny," Loukas replied.

"I will appeal to Destiny; her son Ilion, the Sun; and her daughter Luna, the Moon, to save me from my disgrace. I pray they will help me overcome the loss I suffered because of my hateful pride."

"Such a pity, sir," said the sister with a towering shock of shaggy, coal-black hair.

"Allow us to inform you that Destiny, Sun, and Moon are not easily won over," she warned.

"Time upon time, my sisters and I have joined our mother, Kallo, to plead with Destiny, Sun, and Moon to bless us with the miracle of true love," explained the crimson-haired sister.

"Again, and yet again, we have sought the approval of that hard-hearted trio," said the sister with deep scraggly green hair, the color of seaweed. Regret filtered through her every word.

"But nothing..." offered the black-haired sister, with a loud sigh.

"Yet, if you still have it in mind to petition Destiny, Moon, and Sun for deliverance from your disgrace," the black-haired sister told him, "then you must head due north and look for the mother, son, and daughter in their dazzling vermilion palace."

"And when you come to that hallowed place, let them hear of the flame of desire that burns eternal in our hearts," implored the crimson-haired sister.

In one tender voice, the sisters softly sang their prayer of longing:

"O, Destiny, O Sun, O Moon,
May your wisdom our happiness favor,
To each of us grant a sacred union to savor,
Inspired by love eternally kept sublime,
Forged into bliss by your grand design."

Bringing his hands to his lips, Loukas bowed to the sisters' bidding. He promised to stand before Destiny, Moon, and Sun with the sisters' request, should he ever wander into the hallowed presence of the fearsome mother, daughter, and son.

At their farewell, the sisters offered Loukas a sprig of dried heather and a sackful of bread, cheese, and olives. He thanked them and pointed himself due north to once again take up his quest.

"May courage be your compass," the red-haired sister called to him.

"May caution be your guide," cried the black-haired sister.

"And may good fortune be your reward," declared the three in one voice.

L oukas pressed onward. From time to time, he reached into his satchel and took out his flute. As he moved briskly down the path, he settled on playing a cheerful tune to fight off his fear of Destiny's rejection. One of his favorite songs followed the adventurous journey of a wandering seafarer on his way homeward.

Loukas smiled, recalling happy times when Lambros danced to the seafarer's joyful story. Whenever Loukas played the song, the snake never failed to sway to the music's changing chords.

Will I ever again find the peace and happiness that came into my life when Lambros and I became friends? Loukas thought, sadly.

Just as the sun was edging toward the day's zenith, Loukas stopped to rest in a grove of olive trees. No sooner had he settled onto the cool earth than a raggedy giant came barreling down the path and stood over him, snorting. The giant dwarfed Loukas with its huge body.

"What brings you to this forsaken place where even the egret rarely flies?" the giant asked in a thunderous voice. It studied Loukas with large, soulful eyes.

Jolted backward from the giant's explosive greeting, Loukas surveyed its hulking appearance.

The giant's facial features reminded Loukas of a frog's curious expression. In place of hands and arms, the giant had gangly flippers. Brown algae covered its webbed feet. Topping its head was an untamed mane of green reeds. It wore a threadbare cloak with a patchwork display of underwater plants and creatures. An odor of sulfur hovered over its massive frame.

"My friend," replied Loukas, cowering from the giant's sheer bulk, "I'm on my way to Destiny's palace. I will seek the advice of Destiny and her son Ilion, the Sun, and her daughter Luna, the Moon, to show me the way to mend my broken heart and turn my ruined life around."

"You poor man," roared the giant. "No one knows better than me that the mercy you expect from that fickle family is denied far more times than it is given. Look around you," it howled. It grimaced with disgust as it waved a flipper over the parched, cracked riverbed.

"Time after time I have begged Destiny for rains to get my river flowing. Again, and yet again, I have pleaded for relief from the drought that has dried up this entire valley. But nothing!" mourned the giant.

"You, though, you're thinking you'll strike a bargain with those cunning soothsayers," the giant bellowed.

Well, then, if Loukas still believed he could sway Destiny and her son and daughter to free him of his suffering, he must be on his way into the northern woods.

"Sooner or later," the giant said, "you will arrive at the glowing vermilion palace where that troublesome family has lived since long before the beginning of earthly time. Should you meet up with that mischievous mother and her untrustworthy offspring, speak to them about me. Tell them Kimon, the river spirit, lives forever with the hope of bringing his waterway back to life."

Drawing himself up to his fullest height, Kimon poured out his prayer of yearning for relief:

"That your design, O sacred sages, these currents may you favor,
To quench with rains the Earth will surely savor,
Thus every living thing may once more thrive,
A grateful chorus chanting, 'Alive! Alive! Alive!'"

Before taking his leave, Loukas nodded his promise to bring Kimon's case before Destiny, Sun, and Moon—if only he could be sure that one day soon he would find himself speaking his heart and mind to them.

At Loukas's farewell, Kimon bent low and handed him a cluster of myrtle leaves. Loukas offered his gratitude with a smile.

Watching Loukas wander off, Kimon called to him in a full-throated voice: "May courage be your compass, caution your guide, and good fortune your reward."

As Loukas took up his search, he cheered himself on by playing the refrain from the "Song of the Racing Dolphins" on his flute. The song called to mind the times Lambros followed the tune's quickening rhythm with lively movements. The memory comforted Loukas.

With his sandals wearing thin, Loukas slowed his pace. He walked along high roads and low roads, the air fragrant with the scent of sweet-smelling wild mint.

Later that day, as sunlight drained away, Loukas climbed a winding path toward a swath of mountains shrouded by a mantle of clouds.

At the trail's summit, the ground's violent quaking pitched Loukas forward. He fell headlong onto the rocky terrain and crawled along the shaking path until he came to a stand of trees.

Once he steadied himself against a tree trunk, he searched for the source of the tremors.

When his vision cleared, Loukas drew in a heavy breath. At a stone's throw beyond him, he saw two facing mountains groaning from a clumsy move to reach each other across the path. The second they came within inches of colliding, they backed off a short distance only to start heaving themselves forward for another face-off.

Loukas staggered across the trembling ground, eager to make a mad dash through the narrow opening the mountains left in their retreat.

But, no! Just as he was about to make his escape and avoid being crushed, the mountains yelled to him above the steady rumble of their unstable movement.

"What brings you to this dismal place where even the gull rarely flies?" cried the mountain to the left of Loukas.

"Your majesties," shouted Loukas, cupping his hands over his ears to weaken the harsh grinding, "I am roaming the highway in search of Destiny; her son Ilion, the Sun; and her daughter Luna, the Moon. It is their wisdom I seek to show me how to mend my broken heart and turn my ruined life around."

"Just as you are desperate to be delivered from your pain," shouted the mountain to Loukas's left, "we long to put an end to the humiliation of this ceaseless heaving forward and backward, backward and forward, again and again and again."

"We have appealed to that merciless mother time after time, pleading with her and her son and daughter to show us the respect we have earned," yelled the mountain toiling to approach from Loukas's right. Its scratchy voice rankled with smoldering rage.

"Time and time again, we've asked to be released from our hideous confinement and restored to our renowned place within nature," the left

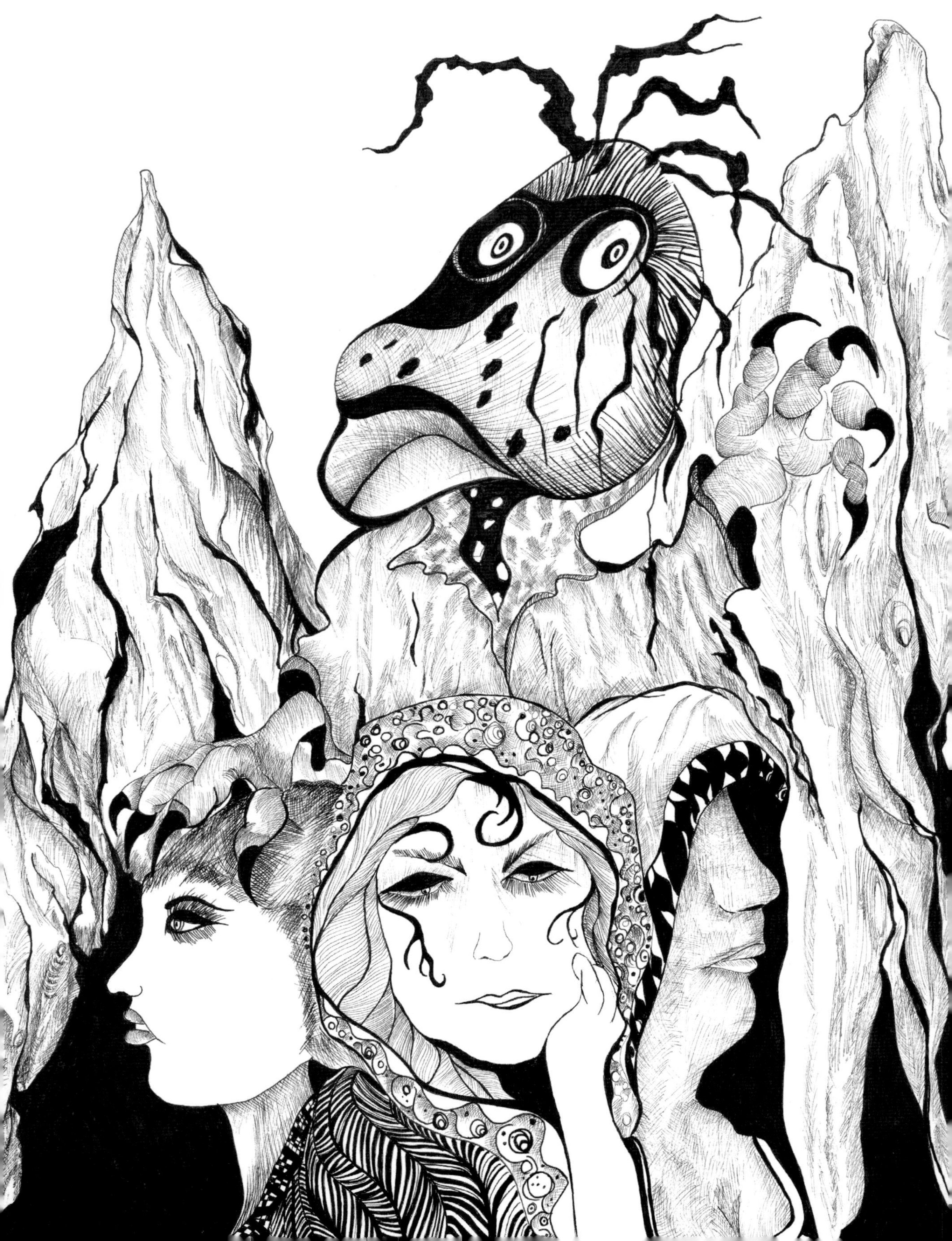

mountain moaned. "But nothing! Never does relief come our way!"

Loukas called out to the pair at the top of his voice, asking for a safe passage so he might try his luck at winning over Destiny's pity.

Like the other tormented souls Loukas had met since entering the forest, the mountains told him he would find that family of unpredictable fortune tellers by traveling northward to their dazzling vermilion palace.

Once there, Loukas should remind Destiny, Sun, and Moon that the desperate mountains at Meander Pass yearn to stand serene and majestic once again.

Joining together, the mountains rasped the prayer of desire Loukas should recite to the infamous mother, son, and daughter when he stood before them:

"Would that your plan our dignity may favor,
Standing firm and noble, admirers of every breed may savor
Our bountiful valleys, woodlands, ancient mythical streams,
Our scented meadows, our craggy cliffs, our mystical fields of dreams."

As Loukas prepared to resume his journey, a spray of purple amaranth flowers floated downward within his reach. He put the savory gift in his satchel and waited for the mountains to retreat. As soon as they began to teeter backward, Loukas ran at breakneck speed through the gap they left in their wake. His feet ached from the sandals' growing discomfort.

"May courage be your compass," called the mountain on the right.

"May caution be your guide," cried the mountain on the left.

"And may good fortune be your reward," howled the mountains in unison.

Without glancing backward, Loukas hurried on down the path as dusk was settling in.

Yet again, the night forest slowly came alive with a steady ruckus of yapping, hissing, and hoot-hoot-hooting.

As the moonless night wore on, Loukas took up courage in both hands and played on his flute the ballad of a legendary sailor's return home after months of hardship on the high seas—yet another song his friend the snake had taken to with great charm.

At dawn's first light, Loukas plodded wearily up a steep ridge. A clot of black clouds rolled in from the north on a gust of foul-smelling wind. Coming to the summit, he stopped and cringed at the sight of the blighted countryside below him.

Squinting, Loukas gazed upon fields of rotting cypresses looming over groves of grotesquely withered olive trees and the stumps of fallen palms. Skeletons of birds lay strewn about the cracked earth from which rose a vapor so putrid that Loukas was forced to press his hands over his nose and mouth. He feared this dreaded wasteland might be an omen foretelling Destiny's refusal to help him bring order to his sorrowful life.

A dreadful thought crossed his mind: *Should I abandon my quest and turn back now and live the rest of my days lonely and grieving my losses?*

"No," he answered aloud. "I will accept the uncertainty of my fate and move forward with hope."

Once again, Loukas strode with wide steps along the pathway. He walked on and on, along hillsides and mountainsides, through valleys and canyons. On and on he walked until blisters formed on the heels of his feet and each step he took sparked a flame of pain.

With the sun just beginning its westward descent, Loukas started to descend into a valley swathed in a thick veil of bluish vapor. A dull trail of light in the distance was drawing him forward when the vapor lifted and a shower of sunlight bathed him in its golden radiance.

Loukas peered through hands that shielded his eyes from the sun's fierce glare. The colossal facade of Destiny's vermilion palace slowly came into focus. He let out a shuddering breath and climbed the marble steps that brought him to a soaring wooden door.

He stared at the door. His heart was pounding. Minutes passed. He sighed, grabbed the metal knocker, and struck the door with three hard thuds.

And then he waited.

Again, he knocked...and waited.

And yet again...

With his hope fading, the palace door suddenly wrenched open.

Destiny withdrew from the shadows. She was unusually tall. She radiated the stately manner of one privileged by royalty. A cavernous dark blue hood concealed her face. She was clothed in a purple tunic of loosely layered silks that reached to her ankles. The garment was embellished with images of planets, stars, suns, and moons sown in crimson floss. Scattered throughout the tunic's oversized sleeves were embroidered medallions displaying a red glass eye in the center of two small, overlapping silver wings. Her jeweled fingers revealed her dark brown skin. She held a black onyx scepter studded with lapis lazuli stones and tipped with an enlarged replica of the medallion found on her sleeves.

Destiny stared quizzically at Loukas.

"Tell it true or not at all," Destiny said in a soft but commanding voice. "What brings you to this hallowed place where humans fear to tread?" she asked.

"Pity me, oh, pity me, your grace," cried Loukas, dropping his gaze and kneeling before Destiny. "I come to you racked with shame, but fired by hope. Save me, revered truth teller. Accept my remorse and rescue me from the dishonorable course my life has taken. Help me to find my way back to the

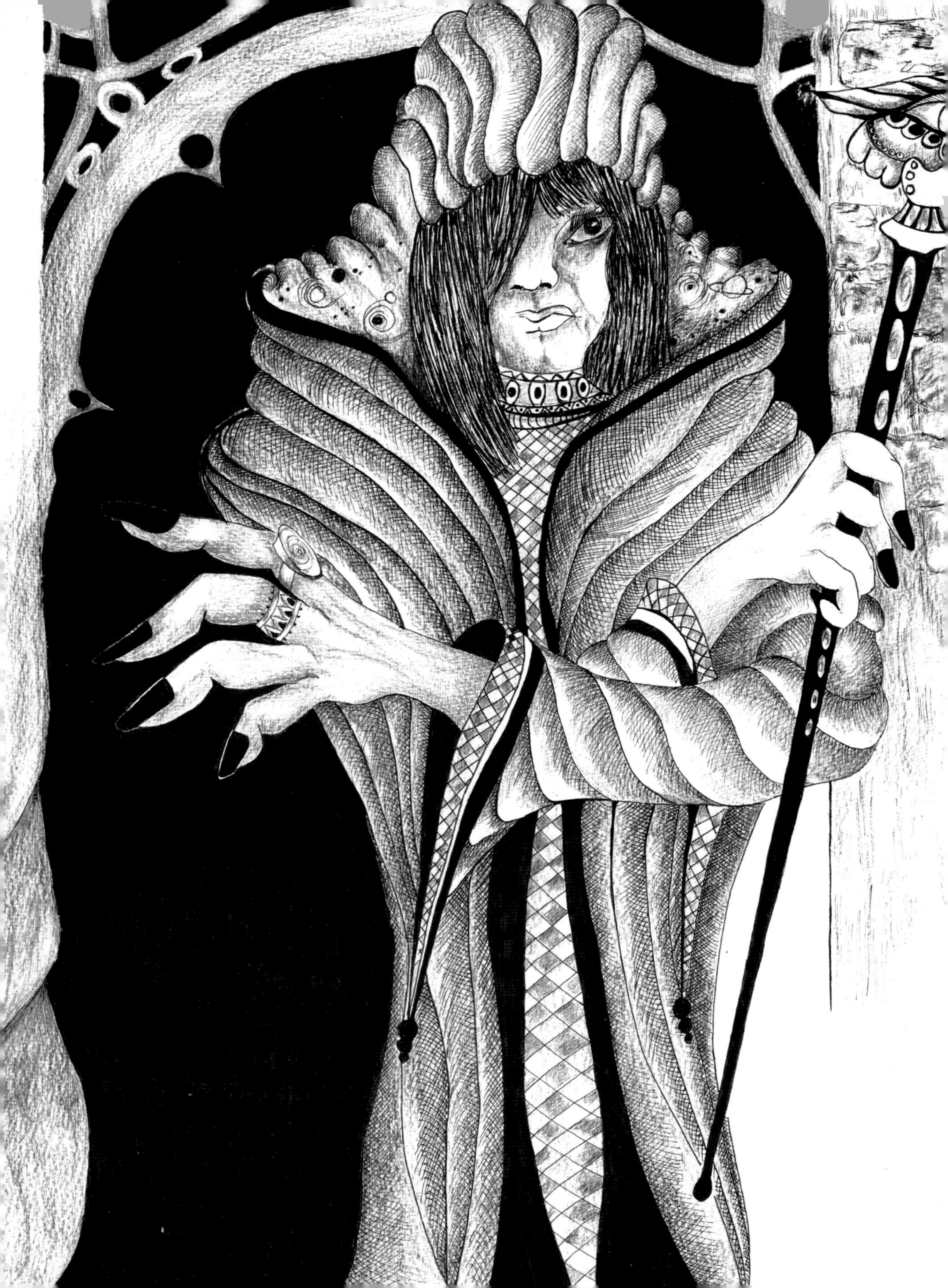

blessings I recklessly squandered."

"Ah, my misguided mortal," Destiny said. She gestured for Loukas to stand. "The favor you seek will only be given if you meet one condition."

"A condition, Your Highness?" Loukas asked.

"My son Ilion, the Sun, and my daughter Luna, the Moon, must join me to decide if you are deserving of our compassion," Destiny said.

"In my mind's eye, I watched you sacrifice the good life designed for you since before timeless time—a life created for you not by happenstance, mind you, but at my bidding," Destiny said, peering at Loukas. "I watched you sink into the depths of pride. You dared to defile my sacred plan and fell under the spell of a trivial game of chance."

Destiny then warned Loukas that when Sun returned from his daily labor and Moon from her nightly watch, they would meet with her to judge Loukas's request. Together they would decide if he deserved to be reunited with his family. They would judge his worthiness to reclaim the riches that fate had made it possible for him to gain for sharing his musical gifts with the snake he so willingly befriended.

Loukas flinched at suddenly hearing Destiny recall his relationship with Lambros.

"Be forewarned, my needy wanderer," she cautioned, pity quickening her words. "I predict that Ilion and Luna's plan for your future will be shaped by the mood that has taken hold of them from observing the habits of living beings on Earth.

"If Ilion and Luna witness uncontrolled surges of hatred among the earth dwellers, their disgust with these beings will surely cast a shadow over your request.

"I will keep you hidden until I know that upon their return Ilion and Luna will tolerate a human like yourself. Will they as much as even listen to your plea to bring an end to the misfortune you cast upon yourself and your precious family?"

With her next breath, Destiny tapped Loukas's forehead. At once, he became a gull with pure white plumage. From his perch on Destiny's raised arm, Loukas fluttered his wings rapidly to keep his balance. His squawking calls continued as Destiny entered the palace just as daylight was draining away.

The next thing Loukas knew, he was standing in his human form in a vast chamber. The room was so brightly lit, he was forced to shield his eyes to avoid reeling from the light's intensity.

Once his vision adjusted to the brightness, Loukas was puzzled to see he now wore a white tunic of coarse cotton. A hooded cloak in deep red covered the tunic. His feet had been bandaged and new sandals replaced his worn ones.

Loukas lowered his hood to get a better look at the room. Displayed on the walls were larger versions of the medallions found on Destiny's sleeves and scepter that showed two silver wings overlapping a red glass eye. Gazing upward, he saw a vaulted ceiling covered with the same images of planets, stars, suns, and moons that graced Destiny's tunic.

The moment Loukas stepped forward to examine the marble fountain in the center of the room, a wooden door swung open. In swept Destiny, dressed now in a crimson silk tunic. She had drawn back her blue hood.

Luna and Ilion followed her.

Ilion's yellow-cowled cloak trailed behind him, skimming the shiny marble floor. The loose cloak covered a tunic of soft burlap, the color of rust. Far shorter than his mother, Ilion had a stout build and the broadest shoulders Loukas had ever laid eyes on. Ilion lurched forward with unsteady steps. At every move, his body twitched and swayed slightly from side to side.

Luna wore a dark blue tunic. Images of meteors appeared on light blue panels that fell from the tunic's wide upturned collar to the white-laced hem that brushed her ankles. A halo of glassy volcanic stones within layers of cosmic dust hovered over her spiked white hair. Luna was far taller than Destiny and Ilion. She had large deep-set blue eyes and a silver complexion. With each wide stride she took behind Destiny and Ilion, Luna seemed poised to leap into the air.

Like their mother, Ilion and Luna each carried an onyx scepter. Like their mother's, their scepters were ornamented with lapis lazuli stones. Both scepters were topped with an enlarged replica of the medallion Loukas had seen on the sleeves of Destiny's tunic and scepter and now on the walls of the chamber in which he stood.

At the front of the room, there were three adjacent high-back thrones set on a dark green marble platform.

Loukas stood stark still by the fountain and focused all of his attention on every move and gesture the three celestial guardians made.

Destiny made her way to a throne of dazzling black onyx and took a seat on a cushion of purple damask. She adjusted the red velvet drape that lined the back of the throne. Placed along the edges of the drape were drawings of playing cards used in games of chance.

Destiny's drape had also been decorated with mysterious images that roused Loukas's curiosity.

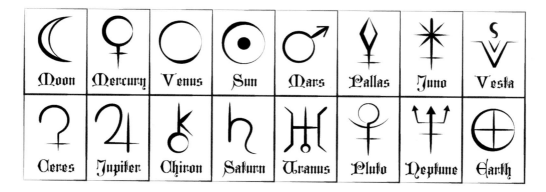

Loukas would later learn from the island's sage that these images are the ones Destiny and her followers consult to foretell the fate of all living beings.

Destiny waved Ilion on to a throne of white marble mottled with black and gray.

Once Ilion sat, he swung his legs over the throne's armrest, sighed deeply, and threw back his cowl. His complexion was the color of a lemon. Color etchings of Ilion in different phases of eclipse and luminosity shimmered in dark red floss on the black drape that fell along the back of his throne. A model of a glowing rainbow arced across the top of Ilion's throne.

At Destiny's bidding, Luna took her place on a throne of blue alabaster. Clear crystal likenesses of Luna's waxing and waning were suspended above her throne. On the dark blue drape that cascaded down the entire length of her throne, images of Luna's eight phases, her cratered surfaces, and her valleys and highlands appeared in circular patterns in thick white yarn.

Luna soon took to singing. Her high-pitched melodies filled the hall with explosions of sound until her song faded into waves of calmer, softer expressions before fading away.

Ilion peered out at Loukas. He scrunched up his face with a steely expression and beckoned to Loukas to move forward.

At the thrones, Loukas genuflected. He slowly stood and raised his head to meet the unflinching scrutiny of mother, daughter, and son. His heart thumped loudly.

Loukas was struck by the ageless beauty of Destiny's face. It was framed by a thick mass of flame-red hair that streamed to midway down her back.

Ilion's body was charged with sudden bursts of quickened movement. Destiny and Luna sat calmly. All three shared a sternness that chilled Loukas through and through.

"Our mother has told us all we need to know about the life you plundered with your arrogance," announced Ilion. He startled Loukas with a voice as agitated as his movements.

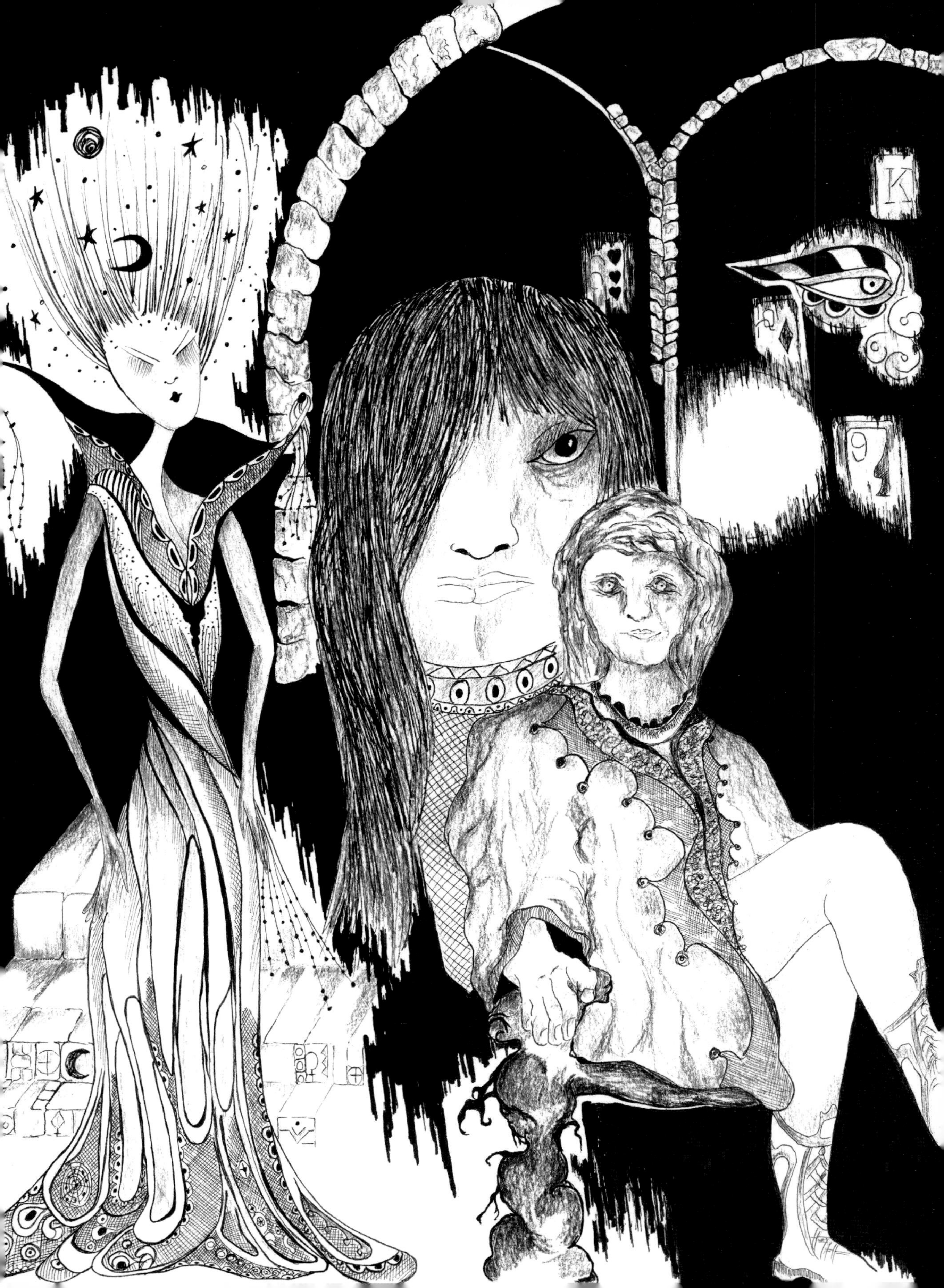
K

"About how you failed to give any thought to the tragic losses pride and greed were leading you toward," Luna sang, grimly.

"About the victims you made of your beloved children and wife," Ilion stammered, suddenly jerking his legs forward and leaning closer to Loukas.

"About your loss of honor," sang Luna.

Had Loukas sensed a hint of sorrow competing with Luna's disapproval? *No,* he came to think. *No mercy to be shown me here. No pity.*

Remorse and shame were taking hold of Loukas when suddenly he was wrenched from the brink of despair by Destiny's verdict.

Had he heard a call that rescued him from the misery he had brought down on himself and his family?

Loukas froze in disbelief, his heart thudding.

"Pardoned, because you attempted an uncertain journey to seek a renewed fate," Destiny said.

"Pardoned, because you have awakened to the error of your ways in placing greediness above love of life and family," Ilion called out, his words a stream of rapid staccato beats.

"Pardoned, because before your fall, you loved the snake that befriended you," sang Luna, rising from her throne.

"A creature reviled by some," Ilion said, "but by you, honored with vibrant harmonies."

"You blessed the snake with the joyfulness of dance and an eternal friendship," said Destiny.

Loukas pressed his hands to his heart. "That snake honored me and my family with his loving concern for our survival," Loukas said, solemnly.

"Now then, return to your village," Destiny advised, "and go directly to the snake's gravesite."

"Dig below the chestnut tree that rises above his grave," Luna sang with a quickened tempo. "There you will find a vast supply of gold coins."

"Take up a hefty amount of the coins, keep the others buried, and then go find the merchant," urged Ilion, pacing vigorously in front of the thrones. "When you come face-to-face with the merchant, stand tall and firm."

Ilion stopped pacing and narrowed his eyes. "With a will sure and steady," Ilion said, his jittery voice stepping over each word, "ask the merchant the direction the Sun takes each and every morning as it spreads its rays."

"'The sun is first seen in the east, of course, where else but in the eastern horizon,' the merchant will surely reply," Ilion predicted. "Now, you sir," continued Ilion, planting himself directly in Loukas's line of vision, "you will contradict the merchant.

"'Oh, no, esteemed merchant, you are sadly mistaken,' you will tell him. Then you will say, 'So certain am I that we can catch sight of the sun rising in our western skies, I am ready to challenge you to a bet to prove the truth of what I am promising.'"

"When the merchant dismisses your claim as nothing more than the blather of a village idiot," Ilion said, twitching, "snare your opponent with an enticing wager. You should jingle the coins in your bag, lean in close to the merchant, and announce: 'You say east, and I say west. Let's put a bet on who is right about the sun's direction, you or me.' And wasting not a minute, you must seal the bet. You must tell the merchant that if he wins, he will receive enough coins to fill a goat's feeding trough. But if you are the victor, you will gain back the entire fortune you had handed over to him at the card game."

"Settle the contest in the village square at dawn on the first cloudless morning after your return," counseled Ilion as he staggered back to his throne. "With your rival by your side, watch for my appearance," Ilion said, slumping into his throne, "the merchant pointed due east, you due west."

"Merciful Ladies, kind-hearted Lord, I lay before you my deepest gratitude," Loukas said, spreading his arms outward.

He then turned and looked for an exit out of the room.

He would begin his journey back to his village.
He would challenge the merchant.
He would win back his blessed life.

No sooner had he started walking toward the wooden door near a set of arched windows than he suddenly stopped.

"The needy ones. I must not forget the pleas of the needy ones I met on my journey to this place," he whispered to himself.

Loukas turned to face Destiny, Luna, and Ilion. Again, he bowed to them.

"Esteemed Ladies, revered Lord, before I take my leave, may I be so bold as to appeal to your bountiful compassion?" he asked, timidly.

"If there be truth to tell, then tell all," replied Destiny.

"While traveling to your realm, I happened upon desperate souls who yearn to have your Ladyship relieve them of their misery," Loukas said.

"Who then, sir?" Destiny asked from her throne.

"Along the forest path, I met Kallo's daughters," Loukas reported.

"'To Destiny, Sun, and Moon,' pleaded the three daughters, 'we humbly offer our earnest desire to be blessed with enduring love.'

"Then together they sang a song of hope:

'O, Destiny, O Sun, O Moon,
May your wisdom our happiness favor,
To each of us grant a sacred union to savor,
Inspired by love eternally kept sublime,
Forged into bliss by your grand design.'"

"Be not deceived by appearance, good fellow," Destiny said. "These sisters are enchantresses. Indeed, they are daughters of a vile sorceress feared among Highlanders as an unscrupulous predator."

"Surely they will take great pleasure holding you hostage for as long as they so desired," sang Luna, gravely.

"Slip past the sisters, slowly crying out, 'I talked with Destiny, Sun, and Moon. They told me to tell you...'" Luna sang, each word drawn out on high-pitched notes.

"But do not tell them our decision about their request until you have moved beyond their reach," ordered Luna, again drawing out her words on even higher notes.

"From a distance, call to them the action they must take to be awarded lasting love," Destiny said.

"You will say, 'By the command of Destiny, Moon, and Sun, sublime love will be awarded the three of you once you cease haunting the humans with terrifying spells,'" Destiny said.

"And then be on your way, swiftly," Luna sang, with short bursts.

Loukas moved to within a few steps of the thrones. He took a deep breath and looked steadily at Destiny before moving his gaze to Ilion and then to Luna.

"On the path I met another desperate soul who seeks a change of fate," Loukas said, barely above a whisper.

"If there be truth to tell, then tell all," Ilion urged.

"From the River Kimon, I bring you a message of grief," Loukas said, his voice growing stronger. "Kimon begs the three of you to take pity on him and end the drought that is ravaging the countryside his waters serve.

"Kimon yearns for the rains that make his river a welcomed source of goodness among the humans who inhabit the valleys and canyons he once passed through. Before I departed from Kimon's parched riverbank, he implored me to recite to you his song of yearning. Kimon cried out:

'That your design, O sacred sages, these currents may you favor,
To quench with rains the Earth will surely savor,
Thus every living thing may once more thrive,
A grateful chorus chanting, 'Alive! Alive! Alive!'"

"You must remain vigilant with Kimon," Ilion cautioned. "In the time it takes an osprey to plunge into the sea," Ilion said, "Kimon has been known to transform the river's tranquil waters into a raging tempest."

"He draws great pleasure from having a storm ravish whatever obstructs the river's tumultuous course," Luna sang, trilling each word.

"As with the sisters," Destiny instructed Loukas, "you must dodge Kimon. Edge out of his sight slowly. At every step, draw out each word, saying, 'I talked with Destiny, Ilion her son, and Luna her daughter.'

"Say not one word more until you have passed beyond the threat of Kimon's deadly temper. Only then should you call to Kimon the warning you have received from us.

"Alert Kimon to our demand. With a strong voice, say: 'River Kimon, saving rains will once again come your way when you vow to control your urge to flood the lowlands with each and every storm.'"

Loukas clasped hands and bowed to Destiny.

After that, he wasted no time bringing up the struggle the mountains at Meander Pass were fated to endure. He told Destiny, Luna, and Ilion of the mountains' agonizing movement toward each other equaled only by their grueling retreat.

Loukas then recited the mountains' plea to be restored to their natural grandeur:

"Would that your plan our dignity may favor,
Standing firm and noble, admirers of every breed may savor
Our bountiful valleys, woodlands, ancient mythical streams,
Our scented meadows, our craggy cliffs, our mystical fields of dreams."

"Whenever these rugged creatures call for help, put aside your trust," Destiny said, scowling.

"So greedy is their craving to dominate nature, they would eagerly sap the life out of anything that breathes and thrives," continued Destiny, her anger rising.

"Nothing must be allowed to compete with their greatness, or so they believe," Destiny said, with a sneer.

"To survive the mountains' treachery, approach Meander Pass as sly as a fox. As soon as the mountains begin to withdraw from one another, race at full speed through the gap they will have left on the path," Destiny advised Loukas.

"Once you are out of harm's way," Luna added with quavering tones, "call out our warning to the mountains in a hearty voice. Say, 'Meander Mountains, if you ever again expect to be admired by the humans and creatures that come your way, you must weaken the power of your storms, your rockfalls, your tremors.' Then, quickly take your leave," Luna sang with one long breath.

With that, Loukas nodded earnestly.

"As it must be, so will it be," Destiny said as she glanced at Loukas.

Moments later, Destiny rose from her throne and made her way to the door through which she had entered the chamber. Ilion and Luna soon followed their mother. When the door opened, all three took their leave.

At once, a tall, bearded man entered the room. He wore a belted tunic of grey cotton that fell to just below his knees. A soft close-fitting black cap covered his head. The large pendant that hung from his neck on a silver chain was a copy of the medallion with the silver wings and red glass eye Loukas had first seen on Destiny's scepter and the sleeves of her tunic.

Loukas was puzzling over the meaning of this curious jewel, when the man gestured for Loukas to follow him.

With long, firm steps, he led Loukas down a wide curving passageway. The sound of their sandals hitting the white marble floor resonated a hollow echo. Loukas's attention was soon drawn to the movement on the domed ceilings. Each dome contained illuminated images of suns, moons, stars, and planets crisscrossing one another in perpetual motion. It dizzied Loukas to stare at them.

Further on, Loukas caught sight of brightly colored tapestries gracing the walls. Each was about the size of the woolen shawls worn by shepherds who tended their flocks in the windswept highlands. The tapestries revealed copies of the playing cards and images found on the drapery that lined Destiny's throne. Placed alongside the tapestries were large versions of the medallion. The medallions' glowing red eyes spread a soft warm light onto the passageway.

The bearded man stopped at a curtained doorway, drew open the curtains, and stepped aside, motioning Loukas to enter a brightly lit room. There was a clear glass table in the center of the room. The table had four stained glass legs in the shape of uncoiled snakes that rose up from the marble floor. The tabletop was set on the heads of the snakes' thick bodies. A black marble chair had been placed next to the table.

A bed made of black wood was set against a white wall to the left of the table. The bed had been made up with several large pillows and a thick, red bedcover. When Loukas finished surveying the room, he noticed that the bearded man had left. Once Loukas settled into the marble chair, fears about his journey back to his village drifted through his mind like gruesome wraiths.

What if the mountains at Meander Pass refuse me a safe passage until I reveal Destiny's decision about their petition? he wondered. *What if River Kimon thrashes me about with deadly gales once he comes to understand the changes Destiny is commanding him to make in his behavior? And the sisters, the three crafty sorcerers. They have the power to trap me in an enchantment so bewitching, I could lose any sense of peace, of direction, of myself.*

A sudden sound at the doorway startled Loukas out of his dread. A trio of tunic-clad attendants strode into the room with platters of food. The pungent aromas spiked Loukas's hunger. He closed his eyes and savored the scents. The smells wafting through the air summoned images of joyful family gatherings where delicious meals brought folks together to celebrate their blessings.

In silence, the attendants served Loukas a meal of traditional island fare. They offered him a mixture of fish and greens in a spiced sauce and grape leaves stuffed with rice, dill, and mint. Another attendant entered the room with a bowl of black and green olives, slices of crusty wheat bread, goat's milk cheese, and assorted fruits.

"Friends," Loukas said to the attendants as he finished the meal with a piece of savory cheese, "I thank you for honoring me with such delicious foods." He reached out to them with open palms.

Several attendants cleared away the remains of the meal. Another poured a sweetly scented drink from an earthenware pitcher into a pewter goblet she had placed on the table.

Then the attendants left the room.

As soon as Loukas swallowed a mouthful of the drink, he grew drowsy. The moment he reached the bed and laid his head on the musk-scented pillow, he drifted into a fitful sleep full of grim visions.

In one dream, Loukas watched his wife Thera scrubbing a floor on her hands and knees. The merchant stood nearby. He contorted his face into a sneer, threw back his head, and let out a grisly laugh. In one swift pivot, he leaped into the air and flew out of the room, waving his arms and cawing like a hawk. Still on her knees, Thera covered her face with her hands and swayed slightly from side to side.

In another dream, Loukas found his children, Sophie and Petros, sitting on the ground in a closure that looked like a cage. They held hands. Loukas could hear them sobbing. At the cage's entrance, a uniformed guard stood rigid and expressionless.

When Loukas's mother and father entered his dream, they stood on a steep hill above the island's harbor with their faces pale and pinched. His father wrung his hands. Not once did they cease scanning the landscape and seascape. His mother called, "Lououououououkasssss, Lououououououkasssss, come home, our dear son, come home."

Loukas now saw Lambros lurching, twitching, and shaking as he moved to the grating sounds of harsh and jarring music. "Help me, oh, pity me," Lambros cried each time the music thrust him into a ragged dance.

In the depth of the night, Loukas heard a voice calling to him. He sat bolt upright, trembling, and squinted into the darkness.

Slowly, a shimmering presence came into focus in the center of the room. Its glow radiated a pleasant warmth that drew Loukas toward it. When Loukas came closer, he found himself standing before the specter of Keeper of the Forest. Keeper placed both hands on Loukas's shoulders. At first Loukas thought he might keel over and fall to the floor. Just as quickly, a surge of courage blazed through him once he met Keeper's warmhearted expression.

As Keeper started to fade, the specter blessed Loukas in a calming voice: "May courage be thy compass, caution thy guide, and good fortune thy reward." Loukas took great comfort from Keeper's fervent words. He gazed at Keeper until his spirit vanished.

At sunup, the same trio of attendants returned to the room. They bore Loukas's satchel and the clothes he had worn on his journey to the palace. One of them stepped forward and gestured Loukas to sit. She set about replacing the bandages that protected his feet with fresh bandages. Another attendant laid before him a parcel of rusks and cheese to take on his journey.

Once the attendants left the room, Loukas dressed and dropped the parcel of food into his satchel.

Moments passed before the bearded attendant returned to the room and beckoned to Loukas to follow him. He led Loukas down a narrow corridor to a massive wooden door. The door was embellished with replicas of the medallion with the silver wings and red glass eye. The bearded attendant knocked once.

"Enter," called Destiny. Loukas grew wide-eyed the moment he stepped into the room. He found Destiny standing in the path of Sun's early morning brilliance filtered through a tall stained glass window. She was bathed in a wavering stream of glowing colors. She invited Loukas to draw nearer.

Loukas struggled to catch his breath as he looked intently at Destiny while moving within her reach. Once he stood before her, he yearned to thank her, Luna, and Ilion for allowing him the hope that some day soon he might once again be blessed with all that he treasured and loved.

When Loukas realized no words could ever express the depth of his gratitude, he held Destiny in a fervent stare. He sighed deeply and raised his palms toward her to show his indebtedness.

"O, mortal wanderer, fare thee well," Destiny said. She placed a hand on each of Loukas's shoulders and met his stare with serene certainty. Loukas would forever hold close to his heart the surge of compassion he felt at Destiny's gentle touch.

Moments later, the bearded attendant returned and dropped to one knee before Destiny. Once he stood, he waved Loukas to follow him. Loukas bowed grave thanks to Destiny and left the room on the heels of the attendant.

Loukas soon stood with the attendant at the head of the path that would lead him back through the forest and then onto the road that would take him to his seaside village.

As Loukas started off, he heard Destiny, Ilion, and Luna singing to him in one compelling voice:

> "May trust light your way.
> May courage be your guide.
> May victory be your reward."

At once, a palace steward poured a bucket of water onto the path to wish Loukas a journey as peaceful as a gently flowing river.

Nearly at a run, Loukas hurried southward. Sometime later, he came to a sudden stop just short of the valley shrouded by a thick curtain of vapor. He recalled coming upon this ghostly place on his way to Destiny's palace. The memory set his heart pounding and pressed him to focus all of his attention on the trials he would have to endure along the path before ever making his way back to his village. When the rising vapors caused Loukas's eyes to sting, he forced himself to sprint past the valley's poisoned air.

Much later, he again came to the stretch of ravaged countryside. As before, he wondered if this horrid wasteland was a harsh omen. Was this place a warning that fate would once more oblige him to forfeit his honor at the hand of the merchant? He shuddered to think of a life bound by fate's whims.

Not long after clearing the wasteland's stench, the path's quaking warned Loukas that beyond the next bend he would find the furious pair of bewitched mountains.

All unfolded according to Ilion's plan. Loukas stumbled off the path and took shelter in a stand of firs where he had a clear view of the mountains' strained movements. As soon as they were wrenched backward, grumbling with each labored thrust, Loukas sprinted through the path's opening.

Loukas's breath came in short bursts as he scuttled to safety. From there, he shouted out Destiny, Sun, and Moon's warning above the mountains' frightful din.

"Listen well, beleaguered mountains of Meander Pass. Destiny, Sun, and Moon have cautioned the two of you to hold to their decree, saying: 'If the pair of you ever again expect to be admired by humans and creatures that come your way, you must weaken the power of your brutish storms, rockfalls, and tremors.'"

"So be it, then," spluttered the mountain on the right, plodding forward.

"Once again that rogue Destiny and her tricksters Sun and Moon have determined to deny us the wonder of satisfying our bold and daring feats," roared the mountain on the left with a lurch.

Relieved to leave the mountains behind, Loukas ran down a steep incline that took him far beyond the pair's hideous struggle.

Later that day, when Ilion had passed his summit, Loukas knew from the ugly stench drifting toward him that the river giant Kimon was close at hand.

As soon as Loukas reached the desolate riverbank, Kimon charged out of the woods and settled on the crest of a steep embankment. His grotesque hulk loomed above Loukas.

"Now then, make haste and come out with it," howled the giant. "What judgment did the cold-hearted tyrants send my way this time, eh?"

"Standing before Destiny, Moon, and Sun, I pleaded for you with the sincerity of a priest," Loukas called at the top of his voice.

"When they came to their decision," continued Loukas as he stumbled up a sheer slope and onto the forest pathway, "they told me to report that the saving rains you crave will once again come your way when you calm your mighty surges and control the currents racing through the lowlands."

Kimon flailed his flippers. He let fly a painful wail that shook trees and sent a tremor through the ground.

Loukas felt the shaking earth as he bolted down the path that took him far from Kimon's madness.

As daylight edged toward dusk, Loukas wended his way through a grassy meadow. A veil of dense fog suddenly shrouded the path.

From within the fog came the voices of the three sisters—ethereal, melodious, inviting.

"Fearless pilgrim, come linger awhile with us. Fear not," the sisters sang in unison. "Oh, do tell the fate Destiny has assigned our desire for blissful love."

Loukas screwed up his face in fear and peered into the fog. "When I told Destiny, Sun, and Moon of your yearning for love, they came together to judge your plea," Loukas cried. He took wide steps backward with the hope of escaping the fog and the sisters' temptation.

"Destiny came forward with a verdict about the love you seek," Loukas said as he tottered into the waning light of the setting sun.

"Truth be told," Loukas called to the sisters, "Destiny issued this decree for you to obey: 'Tell those beguiling enchantresses that enduring love will be theirs to cherish once they cease haunting humans with terrifying enchantments.'"

By the time the sisters' menacing cries caught up with Loukas in a language he did not understand, he was tearing down the path. At that very moment, daylight was seeping from the countryside and the moonless sky was darkening.

Throughout the night, Loukas's heavy footfalls startled creatures he could hear but not see in the darkness. Whimpering critters scampered across his path. Nighthawks screamed as they flew out of their nests. Bats circled overhead, their chirps recalling high-pitched flute vibes.

As dawn moved in, owls' cries drifted through the stillness of the countryside. "TOO-WHIT, TOO-WHIT, TOO-WHIT, TOO-WOO," they called.

Soon after day broke through a cloudy sky, Loukas left the forest and moved on to the road that led directly to his village.

He came to the fork in the road where only a few days earlier he had puzzled over the direction he should take to find Destiny and cast his fate anew. Just as he was about to set off for his village, he was startled to come face to face with Keeper of the Forest.

"Well done, well done," said Keeper, laying a hand on Loukas's shoulder. "Thou most certainly tipped the scale in thy favor. Thou convinced Destiny, Sun, and Moon that thou deserved thar mercy. Oh and oh, they have offered thee the hope of a fate in keeping with the kindness sah thou lived by before a demon took hold of thee.

"Now hurry off to thy village. Abide dah by the plan given thee by Destiny, Sun, and Moon. Find a way oh to live out the rest of thy days close to thy family in peace and loving kindness. So, may it be."

After thanking Keeper, Loukas bounded down the road. He looked neither right nor left, but only straight on until he arrived at Lambros's gravesite. Years ago, Loukas and Thera had set the snake's grave a short distance from their cottage on a bluff that commanded a view of the sea.

It was a blustery day, with strong rushes of wind tearing the sea's surface. Loukas held steady against the trunk of the lofty chestnut tree that rose above the grave. Violent gusts caught the tree's leaves in a frenzied dance.

"Lambros," Loukas cried above the wind's fury, "at Destiny's bidding, dear friend, I come to you with great respect to seek your help."

"Laaaam...bros, Laaaam...bros, Laaaam...bros," Loukas called, competing with the wind's mastery.

Loukas listened and prayed.

When the ground started trembling, Loukas knelt at the base of the tree. He pressed his ear to the ground and covered his other ear with the palm of his hand.

Soon, Loukas began to make out Lambros's scratchy voice.

"Ah, the wonder of your return," croaked Lambros, slowly drawing out each labored word. After a long pause, Lambros continued his gritty speech. "Destiny, Sun, and Moon alerted me to your fall from grace. They told me of your perilous journey to their palace to seek deliverance from your misfortune. From them, I learned of your plan to reclaim a life of happiness, of peace, of love."

"They...may...save...me," Loukas said, his voice vying with yet another angry gust.

"Aye, my friend, just as you once saved my spirit," Lambros said, struggling to be heard. "Over time you consoled me with your soulful music. With dance, the loneliness that darkened my spirit slowly dissolved. With dance, my fears of the violent ways of the humans were soothed."

Once again, Lambros grew silent.

When he was able to speak, he drew on a faint voice and directed Loukas to unearth a mass of coins by digging around the base of the tree. Before long, Loukas would come to a deep pit where he'd find the treasure he was seeking.

"Take what you need to bargain with your merchant," Lambros said, his voice little more than a murmur, "then conceal the pit.

"May you win back your family. May the hidden riches keep you and your kin in good stead for many years to come."

Tears welled in Loukas's eyes as he took up a sharp rock and began scraping away layers of dirt from the tree's base. He was halfway around the tree when a small patch of ground gave way. He raked away the loose dirt with his fingers and discovered a pit similar to the one where he and Thera had found Lambros's dead body years before. This pit was crammed with bulging sacks. Loukas gasped and shook his head from side to side when he saw that each sack overflowed with gold coins.

"Take what you need," Lambros had urged.

Loukas scooped up not one, not two, but *three* handfuls of coins from the nearest sack and put them in his satchel. *Just the amount I need to convince the merchant that the bet could yield him a generous treasure,* Loukas thought.

He covered the pit with loose dirt to conceal the sacks.

Before setting off to find the merchant, Loukas knelt at the base of the tree and thanked Lambros for the treasure. "Dear friend," Loukas called with the wind seizing his words, "in gratitude, I vow to pray each day that your spirit may rest peacefully forever and ever in the comfort of your goodness. So be it."

Instantly, Lambros called back to Loukas from deep within the earth. Once again, Loukas pressed his ear to the ground. He hoped to capture each faint word.

"Courage has served as your compass. Compassion has served as your guide. And now, my music master, may good fortune be your reward," murmured Lambros.

Loukas stood, pressed his hands to his heart, and bowed to his friend. After that, he set off to put forward his wager with the merchant.

Soon enough, Loukas was standing at the entrance of the cottage he had shamefully gambled away. He raised a trembling hand ready to knock, but suddenly stepped away from the door. He drew in a deep, quivering breath, stepped up to the door, and pounded on it three times. Each blow was louder than the one before it.

Loukas smiled at the lady who opened the door a few inches at a time. She narrowed her eyes to scrutinize the caller and returned the smile to see Mr. Loukas standing there. Mr. Loukas was the gentleman she had worked for before becoming the property of the ill-tempered merchant.

Seconds later, the merchant's portly presence filled the doorway as a blast of wind rushed by. The merchant steadied himself, tilted his head slightly to one side, and gave his visitor a devious grin.

"What's at stake?" the merchant asked as he directed Loukas to enter the cottage.

"At stake?" Loukas asked, distracted. He caught himself scouring the entranceway and beyond it for any sign of Thera and the children.

"A bet, sir, a wager," the merchant insisted, "for what other earthly reason would you have dared to pay me a visit if not for—"

"Me to take my chance at winning back all that I have lost to you?" Loukas blurted. His anger about his own foolishness took him off guard. He tamped down the feeling with clenched fists.

"Ha! We shall see, sir," said the merchant. A smirk creased his face. He led Loukas to a cushioned wooden chair next to a table and invited him to sit. He took a seat directly across from his visitor.

Loukas placed his elbows on the table and glared at the merchant. He leaned closer to the man and laid out the terms of the wager.

"If I win," Loukas proposed, "everything and everyone I gave over to you will roll back to me, of course." He spread wide both his arms as though embracing all that he had lost in that devastating card game.

"Of course, of course. And if I win?" the merchant asked.

"You keep all that I handed over to you and as many gold coins as will fill a goat's feeding trough," Loukas said while jingling the coins in his satchel. "And sir, you'll take me for your servant to boot."

"Am I to believe you are a man of means so quickly acquired following your loss?" asked the merchant, facing Loukas down with suspicion. He slowly rubbed his palms together.

"As befits my honor," replied Loukas.

"And what of the contest?" asked the merchant. "At cards, no doubt."

Loukas looked fixedly into his rival's eyes and asked, "Sir, from which earthly direction does the sun first appear each day?"

"Pardon?" the merchant responded, shrugging his shoulders and cupping a hand to his ear.

"The sun, sir, from where does it rise?" repeated Loukas.

"Why, do tell, sir, where else, but from the east?" responded the merchant, smugly.

"You see, esteemed merchant, it has been revealed to me by powers far beyond my own that we will see the sun begin its journey from the west on the next cloudless morning," Loukas announced in a firm and steady voice. "So sure am I that the sun will make its appearance from the west, I am prepared to prove myself right at the risk of losing a hoard of gold coins to win back all that you have rightfully seized from me."

"Well then, if you truly believe you have gained the wisdom to question nature's laws," asserted the merchant, "I'd be a fool not to play along with this preposterous scheme of yours, wouldn't I?"

The merchant leaned in closer to Loukas and spoke. "Yes, yes, of course," he said, "Let's settle this ridiculous wager in the village square the next day that dawns with clear skies. Indeed, we will gather to watch the sun spread its first rays across the *eastern* horizon, of course."

The merchant stood, grabbed onto his chair, and shoved it aside. He pointed Loukas to the front door, opened it, and motioned him to leave. As soon as the door closed, Loukas heard the merchant roaring with deep-throated laughter. Loukas cringed at the sound and took a few brisk steps away from the cottage.

Once outdoors, Loukas wandered awhile through the grounds. He prayed to catch even a glimpse of Thera and his son and daughter. When he found not a trace of them, he moved on down the path with an aching heart.

And so it happened, at dusk on the third day after Loukas's return, a sliver of moon appeared from behind a thin cover of scattered clouds. The moon's appearance held the promise of morning sunlight.

By now, the merchant had spread word of the wager to every villager he had met along the way. He invited each and every one to come to the village square the next morning that dawned with clear skies.

There, the villagers would watch one of their neighbors, Loukas by name, become the laughingstock of the entire island. They would observe him falling prey to his foolhardy claim that the sun would appear on the island not from the east, mind you—the course it had taken since its creation—oh, no, our wise sky gazer was predicting that our old daystar was about to cast its rays from the *western* horizon!

When that morning came with the first signs of a new day dawning, a large crowd of islanders had already been milling about the square. A few vendors were making their way through the square with their carts. They called folks to sample their delicious sweets, fruits, and flavored drinks.

In the center of the square, Loukas and the merchant took their places a short distance from each other on a makeshift wooden platform. The merchant surveyed the eastern horizon. He laid his arms across his chest and smiled. Loukas paced from one end of the platform to the other. He scanned the skyline from east to west and rubbed his hands together. Each of his breaths came in deep and heavy sighs.

Oh, fate of my fate, what chance is there that so miraculous a change in Sun's course could ever happen here in these skies over this humble island? Loukas thought.

He looked out over the crowd.

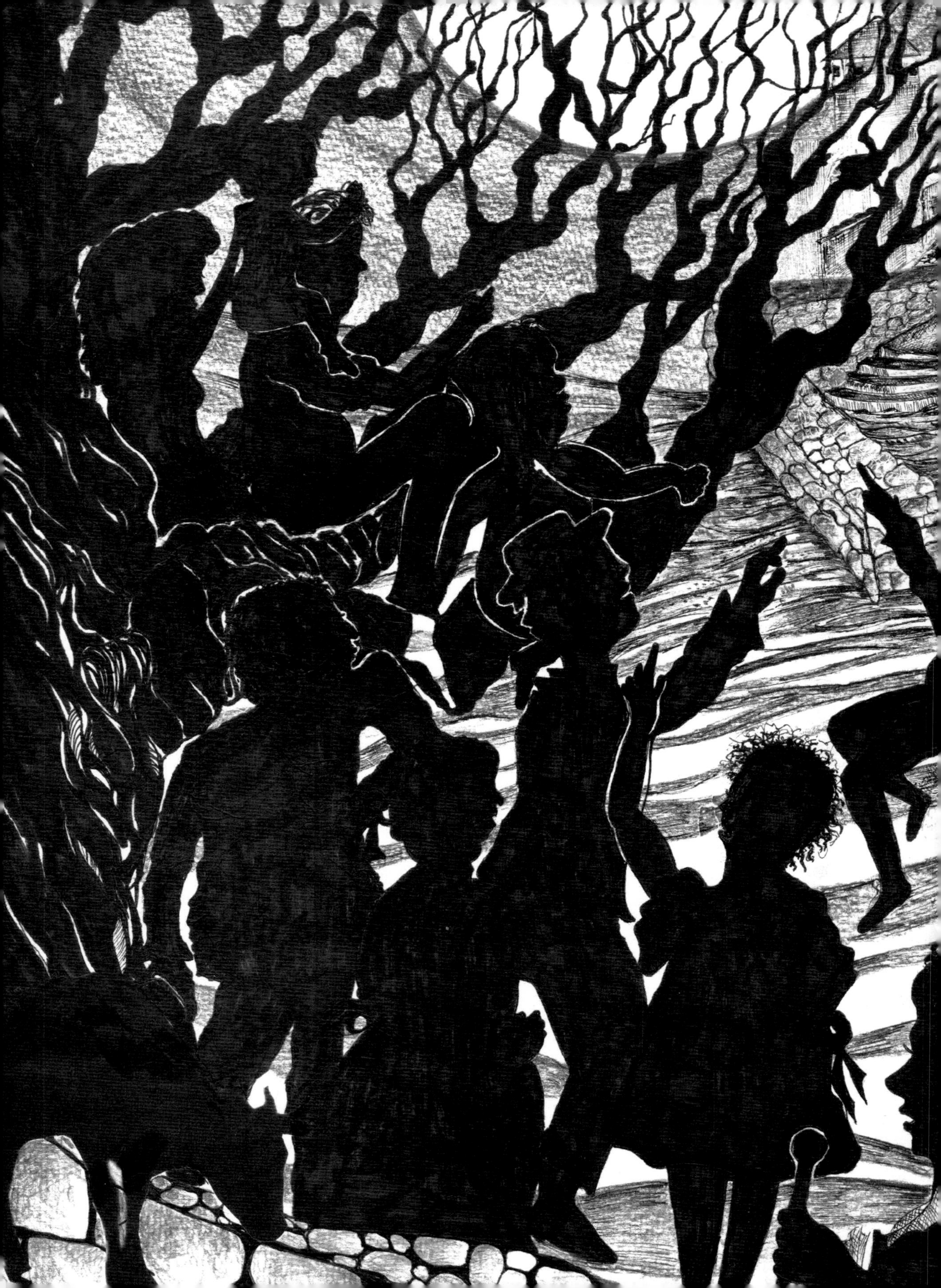

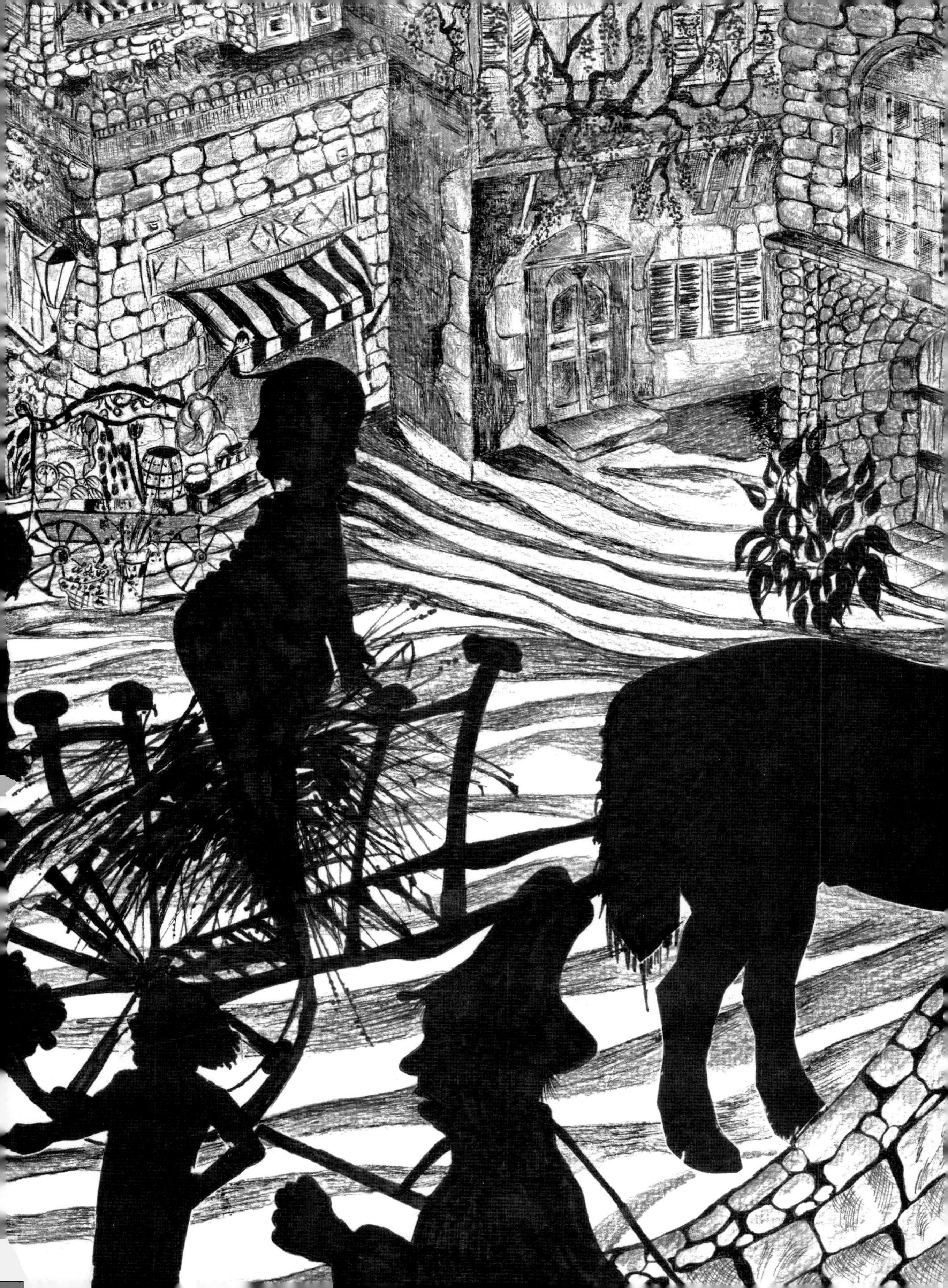

Some islanders had taken to rooftops with their children. From there, a few played at mocking Loukas by calling out outlandish directions for the sun to take.

"From the north," someone shouted.

"No, no, it's the southeast," yelled another.

"The *north*east, you fool," another shouted for all to hear.

Islanders who had climbed onto the branches of an oak that shaded the fountain jeered at Loukas. They pretended they were students who had learned the sun's deepest secrets from their very wise teacher, Mr. Loukas, a famous scientist. They burst into peals of laughter.

Throughout the square, the noise swelled to its loudest pitch.

As the sky grew brighter, the islanders looked to the east.

Suddenly, Sun hurled a needle-thin streak of light out of a narrow break in the dark clouds.

"There it is. There's the sun," yelled a young girl. She pointed to the west and jumped up and down.

"The sun, the sun. It's waking up over there," the girl shouted.

The girl's father took notice of her alarm. He looked westward, ran to a nearby stone bench, climbed on to it, and cried out, "THE SUN IS RISING IN THE WEST!"

Slowly, a hush fell over the crowd. As Sun's glow grew deeper, islanders looked toward the western horizon. Cries of surprise competed with gasps of wonder from one end of the square to the other.

"A miracle," someone called. Others agreed, clapping and cheering.

"A curse, a very bad omen," cried another islander. She fled from the square with her horrified neighbors.

Above the clamor, the merchant could be heard condemning Loukas for using sorcery to disturb a natural wonder. The merchant grumbled, "blasphemy, blasphemy," as he stormed out of the square.

At the very moment the merchant was ranting, Loukas raised his hands, palm against palm, toward the brightening sky. He let fly his whispered songs of praise to Destiny, Ilion, Luna, and Lambros for enabling him to reclaim his dignity.

As soon as Loukas ended his prayers of gratitude, Thera and the children ran to him.

"Papa, Papa," the children cried. They wrapped their arms around their mother and father while the two embraced.

Reaching into his satchel, Loukas brought out the gifts of nature given him by the enchanted sisters, the dried up river, and the raging mountains.

To his son, Petros, he gave the sprig of dried heather. He wished him days of good fortune.

To his daughter, Sophie, he gave the myrtle leaves. He wished her a long and happy life.

To his beloved wife, Thera, he gave the purple amaranth flowers, now dried. He wished her a richness of health from that day forward.

When Loukas's and Thera's parents joined the reunion, the families together sang an earnest prayer of thanks to their God, their saints, and the spirits that watched over them.

When the new day dawned following Sun's momentous performance, Sun resumed casting his energy from east to west. He once again took up the daily cycle assigned him since he first whirled into the galaxy millions of years ago.

As for Loukas, Thera, and the children, for forty days and forty nights they opened their doors and hearts to their neighbors. With their neighbors, they celebrated their blessings with food and drink, and they danced to songs Loukas played on his magical flute.

When the festivities ended, every family member, young and old alike, pledged to desire nothing more than a future endowed with peace, good health, and a favorable destiny.

For generations, islanders have told tales about the fateful game of chance that could have kept Loukas from his family and cast him into deep despair.

They told of Loukas's courageous journey into the depths of the island's forest to beg for mercy and healing from Destiny, Sun, and Moon.

They told of the clemency granted Loukas for his love of family.

They told of the pardon Loukas had received for his devotion to Lambros, the mysterious talking, dancing snake who had brought enduring happiness to Loukas and everyone within Loukas's circle of reverence and respect.

They told of the freedom Loukas gained from Sun's miraculous passage from west to east on a suspenseful day long past.

They told of the songs Loukas had sung from village to village in praise of the lessons he had learned from his loss and recovery.

He had sung the song about pride's power to blur the boundary between right and wrong.

Pride's lure, he had learned, could be weakened through acts of kindness and through sharing his wealth with unfortunate folk.

He had sung the song of awakening to greed's bewitchment.

Greed, he had learned, could be repelled by living each day with deepening gratitude for his revered family, his good fortune, his blessed, renewed fate.

For as long as Loukas lived, he never once took for granted the happy moral life Destiny, Sun, Moon, and Lambros had allowed him to regain and savor.

Author's Note

Loukas and the Game of Chance is based loosely on two Greek folktales. There are different versions of the tales, but they all focus on a character who sets out on a treacherous journey to try to alter his fate after he ruins his life. In every version of the tale, a poor, unnamed character becomes friends with a magical snake. The snake rewards the character's kindness with an endless supply of gold coins because he loves being entertained by the character's flute music. Unfortunately, the character foolishly loses a bet that strips him of his fortune and the family he adores. That's when he takes off on a wild trek through an eerie forest in search of Destiny; her son, the Sun; and her daughter, the Moon. They'll certainly help him win back his fortune, his family, and his honor, won't they?

I had worked on a retelling of one of these tales, "The Snake Tree," for a collection of Greek folktales I co-authored with Soula Mitakidou. After that experience, I kept wondering about the strange relationships and events in the story. I kept returning to the mysterious bond between the snake and the flute-playing boy. What if I gave the snake a background, a heritage, and a community in a far-off realm that could be made known to the boy he befriends? What could the snake, whom I named "Lambros," and the boy, whom I named "Loukas," learn about trust, loyalty, and commitment as their friendship grew through mutual acts of kindness and respect?

Destiny; her son, the Sun; and her daughter, the Moon also sparked my curiosity. In my imagination, they had a lot of power. In two versions of "The Snake Tree," Destiny was simply "a good old lady" or "a middle-aged lady." Yet to me, she appeared elegant, regal, and all-wise. For some storytellers, her son, the Sun, was either a hungry, human-eating ogre or a laid-back guy who's eager to help Loukas regardless of what caused him to become so unlucky. My sun would be tense, jittery, fickle, and arrogant. He could be the kind of son who would easily defy his mother's decision to allow Loukas a better fate and, thus, a better life. Or, he might be in the mood to save Loukas from despairing and send him off with the promise of a good life. The Sun needed to be carefully watched.

Destiny's daughter, the Moon, is a character I invented. She doesn't appear in any of "The Snake Tree" tales I read, and she came into being when Nikki, a member of my writers' group, suggested that the Moon could bring an interesting perspective to Loukas's dilemma and to the tense drama he finds himself in when Destiny, Sun, and Moon put him on trial. From the moment the Moon came to me, I saw her as watchful, opinionated, and, like her mother, fair and just. I always knew Moon should have a gorgeous singing voice.

Keeper of the Forest is another character I invented. He's like the sage folktale characters typically meet on the road right before their quest begins. The sage offers counsel, forewarning, and hope. The hope is given only if the character complies with whatever prophecy the sage offers. In *Loukas and the Game of Chance*, the sage was first cast as a wizard. Then, Donald Babisch, the illustrator of this book, challenged me to develop a sage completely different from the ubiquitous wizard. Enter Keeper of the Forest. This kind-hearted being is part magician, part environmental steward, part protector, part caregiver, and part writer. He also adds a bit of comic relief to an otherwise dark storyline.

When I think about why I wanted to reimagine "The Snake Tree," I always come back to my wish to entertain readers with a story that awakened them to life's struggles and mysteries. I had in mind the inevitability of hard times and loss, as well as how courage and perseverance can open the way to hope and recovery. I also wanted to honor the Greek cultural belief in the power of a story to comfort and give advice. This belief, I discovered, can be traced to the etymology of the Greek word for folktale, *paramythi*, which in turn derives from the archaic Greek verb *paramytheome*, meaning to advise and console.

We're all in good hands among earnest storytellers, writers, and readers.

Further Reading

Ioannou, Georgios, "The Snake Tree," *Ta Paramythia you Laou Mas* [Folktales of Our People]. Athens, Greece: Ermis, 1987.

Kafandaris, Kostas, "The Snake Tree," *Ellinika Laika Paramythia* [Greek Folktales]. Athens, Greece: Odysseas, 1988.

Moskovi, Irini. "The Fisherboy, the Snake, and the Sun," *Paramythia tis Patridas mou* [Folktales of My Country]. Athens, Greece: A. Mavrides, 1953.

Mitakidou, Soula, and Anthony L. Manna, F*olktales from Greece: A Treasury of Delights*. Greenwood Village, CO: Libraries Unlimited, 2002.

About the Author

Anthony L. Manna's first collaboration with Soula Mitakidou, *Mr. Semolina-Semolinus: A Greek Folktale*, illustrated by Giselle Potter, was an ALA-ALSC Notable Book, a Marion Vannett Ridgway Award winner, and a New York Public Library Best Book for Children. Another collaboration of theirs, *The Orphan: A Cinderella Story from Greece*, illustrated by Giselle Potter, was a Bank Street College of Education Best Book of 2012. They also collaborated on the anthology, *Folktales from Greece: A Treasury of Delights*. Anthony has worked with children and teens in drama and storytelling; has been an actor, director of children's theater, vehicle repossessor, and janitor; and has taught in schools and universities in Turkey, Greece, Albania, and the United States. He divides his time between Ohio and Arizona.

About the Illustrator

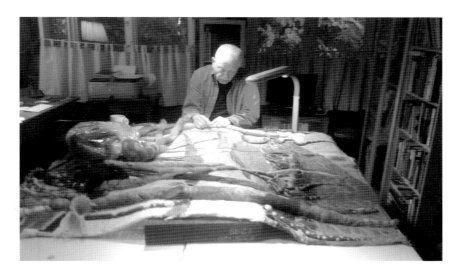

Donald Babisch is an artist and art educator who has worked with children in elementary and middle school. An alumnus of New York University's graduate art education program, he is a former adjunct instructor in the art education program at Youngstown State University in Ohio. The author of articles in several art education journals, Donald is both the author and illustrator of *Who is That Peeking in My Windows?* Having received an Honorable Mention for a felted piece he exhibited at the Crooked Tree Arts Center in 2014, he is now exploring and creating large needle felted portraits, scenes, and allegories. An avid gardener, he lives in a log cabin in northeast Ohio.

Acknowledgments

I am deeply indebted to the children and their teachers in that precious kindergarten in Thessaloniki, Greece, where I was happily researching the children's literacy development in the early 1990s. Much to my delight, that kindergarten classroom proved to be a great setting for discovering the treasures of Greek folklore. Stories were told, read, heard, and dramatized throughout the day, and traditional songs and dances often served as enjoyable transitions between formal lessons. As the children drew me into their daily read-alouds, I became more and more fascinated by the mystery, magic, suspense, and wonder of their folktales and fairy tales. I'll be forever thankful to Niki and Jenni, two extraordinary teachers, for welcoming me into their classroom and for sharing their passion and expertise. Thanks, as well, to those children who readily and patiently worked with me in exploring their experiences as readers and writers while introducing me to a treasure trove of unforgettable stories. *Efharistó!*

My gratitude reaches out to Soula Mitakidou, a professor at Aristotle University of Thessaloniki, who was engaged in a research project in the same kindergarten classroom at the very same time I was engaged in my own. When we realized we shared a love and respect for tradition, particularly for the stories of old, we set out to collaborate on translating and reimagining a selection of the tales with the intention of making them accessible to readers outside of Greece. Over the years, it has been a great joy to sit at the same computer in Thessaloniki or in Ohio or to exchange a story-in-progress across the Atlantic via the internet. Our challenge as folklorists is to mine the mysticism, the captivating and unusual music, and the brilliant folk wisdom of these wondrous tales. Soula has remained a phenomenal culture guide and mentor whose intriguing stories about Greece's landscape, history, and folklore have been instrumental in making this richly endowed country right in the heart of the Mediterranean Sea come alive for me. *Efaristó, tin eidiki fili mou!*

Special thanks are due to the KidLitCrit group—my critique partners—I joined up with here in northeast Ohio. With enduring patience, a seasoned awareness of what it takes to make your story the best one you've ever attempted to write, and a gentle manner of offering suggestions for how to align story content with whatever truth you're pursuing, these writers led me to a much deeper understanding of writerly techniques for building a story that reaches the hearts and minds of readers. Thank you Rebecca Barnhouse, Jacqui Lipton, Nikki Ericksen, and Eliza Osborn—such talented wordsmiths—for cheering me on with your endless support. Blessed am I to have the four of you as my talented and earnest mentors, friends, and collaborators.

I am also grateful for the entire team at Mascot Books. Kristin Perry, Director of Author Services, an incisive copy editor and proofreader who guided me through countless drafts with saintly resolve and quintessential professionalism; Jasmine White, graphics sage, for the book's attractive interior design; Chris Baker, Marketing Manager, an outreach virtuoso, for helping connect the book with booksellers, reviewers, and social media influencers; and all those other Mascot folks, way too many to mention individually—managers, packers, shippers, handlers—who need to be celebrated for keeping the book afloat with such great care. Mascot Books was the perfect home for bringing forth Loukas and his journey to freedom. Thank you all.

A heap of thanks are due to the Szewczuk Ladies of N.J.—Patte, Katya, and Tatiana—for their encouragement and social media savvy, and to Janet Hill who read a very early draft and convinced me to make the setting more vivid, the characters more distinct.

The growth of this book has much to do with Donald Babisch's wisdom. As I moved through numerous drafts, he helped me stay the course when I couldn't find the path, and his super smart suggestions for character, theme, and style often awakened me to what lurked beneath or beyond the version of the tale I happened to be constructing at the moment. Thank you for taking time away from your art—your prized felted works—to buoy me up and to help me hone my craft while you were also deeply involved in making the stirring pen and ink illustrations that enliven Loukas's story all the way through. *Duzhe tobi dyakuyu.*